Constance Cary Harrison

Short Stories

Constance Cary Harrison

Short Stories

ISBN/EAN: 9783744707916

Printed in Europe, USA, Canada, Australia, Japan

Cover: Foto ©Andreas Hilbeck / pixelio.de

More available books at **www.hansebooks.com**

SHORT STORIES

EDITED BY

CONSTANCE CARY HARRISON

NEW YORK -
HARPER & BROTHERS PUBLISHERS
MDCCCXCIII

NOTE.

MRS. STODDARD'S "My Own Story" was published in *The Atlantic Monthly;* Miss Chesebro's "In Honor Bound" and Mrs. Slosson's "A Speakin' Ghost" appeared in *Harper's Magazine;* Miss Crosby's "An Islander" was first printed in *Scribner's Magazine;* and Mrs. Harrison's "Monsieur Alcibiade" is reprinted from *The Century Magazine.*

CONTENTS.

INTRODUCTION.

THE series of collections of which this volume
is a part is made up of representative work of
the women of the State of New York in period-
ical literature.

This literature has been classified under its
conspicuous divisions—Poetry, Fiction, History,
Art, Biography, Translation, Literary Criticism,
and the like.

A woman of eminent success in each department has then been asked to make a collection
of representative work in that department, to
include in it an example of her own work, and
to place her name upon the volume as its
Editor.

These selections have been made, as far as
possible, chronologically, beginning with the
earliest work of the century, in order that
the volumes may carry out the plan of the

"Exhibit of Women's Work in Literature in the State of New York," of which they are an original part.

The aim of this Exhibit was to make for the Columbian Exposition a record of literary work, limited, through necessity, both by sex and locality, but, as far as possible, accurate and complete, and to preserve this record in the State Library in the Capitol at Albany.

It includes twenty-five hundred books, beginning with the works of Charlotte Ramsay Lennox, the first-born female author of the province of New York, published in London in 1752, closing with the pages of a translation of Herder, still wet from the press, and comprising the works of almost every author in the intervening one hundred and forty years.

It includes also three hundred papers read before the literary clubs of the State, a summary of the work of all writers for the press, and the folios which preserve the work of many able women who have not published books.

The women of the State of New York have had the honor of decorating and furnishing the Library of the Woman's Building. Believing the best equipment of a library to be literature, they have therefore prepared this Exhibit, and have made its character comprehensive and historic, in order that it may not be temporary, but that it may be preserved in the State Library and may have permanent value for future lovers and students of Americana.

In the preparation of these volumes Messrs. Harper & Brothers have arranged that the composition and other mechanical work, as well as the designing of the cover, should be done by women, thus giving especial significance to the title, "The Distaff Series."

BLANCHE WILDER BELLAMY,
*Chairman of the Committee on Literature
of the Board of Women Managers of the
State of New York.*

SHORT STORIES.

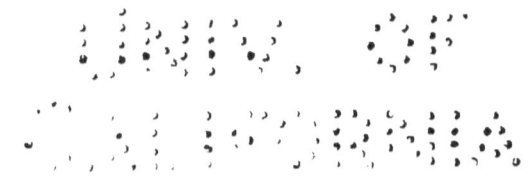

MY OWN STORY.

BY

MRS. ELIZABETH DEAN BARSTOW STODDARD.

"Oh, tell her, brief is life, but love is long."

" WHAT have I got that you would like to have? Your letters are tied up and directed to you. Mother will give them to you when she finds them in my desk. I could execute my last will myself, if it were not for giving her additional pain. I will leave everything for her to do except this: take these letters, and when I am dead give them to Frank. There is not a reproach in them, and they are full of wit; but he won't laugh when he reads them again. Choose now, what will you have of mine?"

"Well," I said, "give me the gold pen-holder that Redmond sent you after he went away."

Laura rose up in her bed and seized me by my shoulder and shook me, crying between her teeth. "You love him! you love

I

him!" Then she fell back on her pillow.
"Oh, if he were here now! He went, I
say, to marry the woman he was engaged
to before he saw you. He was nearly mad,
though, when he went. The night mother
gave them their last party, when you wore
your black lace dress, and had pink roses in
your hair, somehow I hardly knew you that
night. I was in the little parlor, looking
at the flowers on the mantel-piece, when
Redmond came into the room, and, rushing
up to me, bent down and whispered, 'Did
you see her go? I shall see her no more;
she is walking on the beach with Maurice.'
He sighed so loud that I felt embarrassed,
for I was afraid that Harry Lothrop, who
was laughing and talking in a corner with
two or three men, would hear him; but he
was not aware that they were there. I did
not know what to do, unless I ridiculed
him. 'Follow them,' I said. 'Step on her
flounces, and Maurice will have a chance to
humiliate you with some of his cutting, exquisite politeness.' He never answered a
word, and I would not look at him; but
presently I understood that there were tears
falling. Oh, you need not look towards me
with such longing; he does not cry for you
now. They seemed to bring him to his

senses. He stamped his foot; but the carpet was thick; it only made a thud. Then he buttoned his coat, giving himself a violent twist as he did it, and looked at me with such a haughty composure that, if I had been you, I should have trembled in my shoes. He walked across the room towards the group of men. 'Ah, Harry,' he said, 'where is Maurice?' 'Don't you know?' they all cried out; 'he has gone as Miss Denham's escort.' 'By Jove!' said Harry Lothrop, 'Miss Denham was as handsome as Cleopatra to-night. Little Maurice is now singing to her. Did he take his guitar under his arm? It was here, for I saw a green bag near his hat when we came in to-night.' Just then we heard the twang of a guitar under the window, and Redmond, in spite of himself, could not help a grimace. Is it not a droll world?" said Laura, after a pause; "things come about so contrariwise."

She laughed such a shrill laugh that I shuddered to hear it, and I fell a-crying.

"But," she continued, "I am going, I trust, where a key will be given me for this cipher."

Tears came into her eyes, and an expression of gentleness filled her face.

"It is strange," she said, "when I know

that I must die, that I should be so moved by earthly passions and so interested in earthly-speculations. My heart suppplicates God for peace and patience, and at the same moment my thoughts float away in dreams of the past. I shall soon be wiser; I am convinced of that. The doctrine of compensation extends beyond this world; if it be not so, why should I die at twenty, with all this mysterious suffering of soul? You must not wonder over me, when I am gone, and ask yourself, 'Why did she live?' Believe that I shall know why I lived, and let it suffice you and encourage you to go on bravely. Live and make your powers felt. Your nature is affluent, and you may yet learn how to be happy."

She sighed softly, and turned her face to the wall, and moved her fingers as sick people do. She waited for me to cease weeping; my tears rained over my face so that I could neither see nor speak.

After I had become calmer, she moved towards me again and took my hand; her own trembled.

"It is for the last time, Margaret. My good, skilful father gives me no medicine now. My sisters have come home; they sit about the house like mourners, with idle hands, and do not speak with each other. It is terrible, but it will soon be over."

She pulled at my hand for me to rise. I staggered up, and met her eyes. Mine were dry now.

"Do not come here again. It will be enough for my family to look at my coffin. I feel better to think you will be spared the pain."

I nodded.

"Good-bye!"

A sob broke in her throat.

"Margaret"—she spoke like a little child —"I am going to heaven."

I kissed her, but I was blind and dumb. I lifted her half out of the bed. She clasped her frail arms round me, and hid her face in my bosom.

"Oh, I love you!" she said.

Her heart gave such a violent plunge that I felt it, and laid her back quickly. She waved her hand to me with a determined smile. I reached the door, still looking at her, crossed the dark threshold, and passed out of the house. The bold sunshine smote my face, and the insolent wind played about me. The whole earth was as brilliant and joyous as if it had never been furrowed by graves.

Laura lived some days after my interview with her. She sent me no message, and I did not go to see her. From the garret windows of our house, which was half a mile distant from Laura's, I could see the windows of the room where she was lying. Three tall poplar-trees intervened in the landscape. I thought they stood motionless so that they might not intercept my view while I watched the house of death. One morning I saw that the blinds had been thrown back and the windows opened. I knew then that Laura was dead.

The day after the funeral I gave Frank his letters, his miniature, and the locket which held a ring of his hair.

"Is there a fire?" he asked, when I gave them to him; "I want to burn these things."

I went to another room with him.

"I'll leave everything here to-day, and may I never see this cursed place again! Did she die, do you know, because I held her promise that she would be my wife?"

He threw the papers into the grate, and crowded them down with his boot, and watched them till the last blackened flake disappeared. He then took from his neck a hair chain, and threw that into the fire also.

"It is all done now," he said.

He shook my hand with a firm grasp and left me.

A month later Laura's mother sent me a package containing two bundles of letters. It startled me to see that the direction was dated before she was taken ill: "To be given to Margaret in case of my death. June 5th, 1848." They were my letters, and those which she had received from Harry Lothrop. On this envelope was written, "Put these into the black box he gave you." The gold pen-holder came into my hands also. *Departure* was engraved on the handle, and Laura's initials were cut in an emerald in its top. The black box was an ebony, gold-plated toy, which Harry Lothrop had given me at the same time Redmond gave Laura the pen-holder. It was when they went away, after a whole summer's visit in our little town, the year before. I locked the letters in the black box, and,

"Whether from reason or from impulse only,"

I know not, but I was prompted to write a line to Harry Lothrop.

"Do not," I said, "write Laura any more letters. Those you have already written to her are in my keeping, for she is dead. Was it not a pleasant summer we passed together? The second autumn is already at hand; time flies the same, whether we are dull or gay. For all this period what remains except the poor harvest of a few letters?"

I received in answer an incoherent and agitated letter. What was the matter with Laura? he asked. He had not heard from her for months. Had any rupture occurred between her and her friend Frank? Did I suppose she was ever unhappy? He was shocked at the news, and said he must come and learn the particulars of the event. He thanked me for my note, and begged me to believe how sincere was his friendship for my poor friend.

"Redmond," he continued, "is for the present attached to the engineer corps to which I belong, and he has offered to take charge of my business while I am a day or two absent. He is in my room at this moment, holding your note in his hand, and appears painfully disturbed."

It was now a little past the time of year when Redmond and Harry Lothrop had left us—early autumn. After their departure Laura and I had been sentimental enough

to talk over the events of their visit. Re-
calling these associations, we created an
illusion of pleasure which of course could
not last. Harry Lothrop wrote to Laura,
but the correspondence declined and died.
As time passed on we talked less and less of
our visitors, and finally ceased to speak of
them. Neither of us knew or suspected the
other of any deep or lasting feeling towards
the two friends. Laura knew Redmond
better than I did—at least, she saw him
oftener; in fact, she knew both in a different way. They had visited her alone,
while I had met them almost entirely in
society. I never found so much time to
spare as she seemed to have, for everybody
liked her, and everybody sought her. As
often as we had talked over our acquaintance, she was wary of speaking of Redmond. Her last conversation with me revealed her thoughts, and awakened feelings
which I thought I had buffeted down. The
tone of Harry Lothrop's note perplexed me,
and I found myself drifting back into an old
state of mind I had reason to dread.

As I said, the autumn had come round.
Its quiet days, its sombre nights, filled my
soul with melancholy. The lonesome moan
of the sea and the waiting stillness of the

woods were just the same a year ago; but Laura was dead, and Nature grieved me. Yet none of us are in one mood long, and at this very time there were intervals when I found something delicious in life, either in myself or the atmosphere.

> "Moreover, something is or seems
> That touches me with mystic gleams."

A golden morning, a starry night, the azure round of the sky, the undulating horizon of sea, the blue haze which rose and fell over the distant hills, the freshness of youth, the power of beauty—all gave me deep voluptuous dreams.

I can afford to confess that I possessed beauty; for half my faults and miseries arose from the fact of my being beautiful. I was not vain, but as conscious of my beauty as I was of that of a flower, and sometimes it intoxicated me. For in spite of the comforting novels of the Jane Eyre school, it is hardly possible to set an undue value upon beauty; it defies ennui.

As I expected, Harry Lothrop came to see me. The sad remembrance of Laura's death prevented any ceremony between us; we met as old acquaintances, of course, although we had never conversed together half an

hour without interruption. I began with
the theme of Laura's illness and death, and
the relation which she had held towards me.
All at once I discovered, without evidence,
that he was indifferent to what I was saying; but I talked on mechanically, and like
a phantasm the truth came to my mind.
The real man was there—not the one I had
carelessly looked at and known through
Laura.

I became silent.

He twisted his fingers in the fringe of my
scarf, which had fallen off, and I watched
them.

"Why," I abruptly asked, "have I not
known you before?"

He let go the fringe, and folded his hands,
and in a dreamy voice replied,

"Redmond admires you."

"What a pity!" I said. "And you—you
admire me, or yourself, just now; which?"

He flushed slightly, but continued with a
bland voice, which irritated and interested
me:

"All that time I was so near you, and you
scarcely saw me; what a chance I had to
study you! Your friend was intelligent and
sympathetic, so we struck a league of friendship: I could dare so much with her, be-

cause I knew that she was engaged to marry
Mr. Ballard. I own that I have been troubled about her since I went away. How
odd it is that I am here alone with you in
this room! how many times I have wished
it! I liked you best here; and while absent
the remembrance of it has been inseparable
from the remembrance of you—a picture
within a picture. I know all that the room
contains: the white vases, and the wire bas-
kets, with pots of Egyptian lilies and dam-
ask roses, the books bound in green and
gold, the engravings of nymphs and fauns,
the crimson bars in the carpet, the flowers
on the cushions, and, best of all, the arched
window and its low seat. But I had promised myself never to see you; it was all I
could do for Laura. She is dead, and I am
here."

I rose and walked to the window, and
looked out on the misty sea, and felt
strangely.

"Another lover," I thought, "and Redmond's friend, and Laura's. But it all be-
longs to the comedy we play."

He came to where I stood.

"I know you so well," he said—"your
pride, your self-control, even your foibles;
but they attract one, too. You did not es-

cape heart-whole from Redmond's influence.
He is not married yet, but he will be; he is
a chivalrous fellow. It was a desperate
matter between you two—a hand-to-hand
struggle. It is over with you both, I believe: you are something alike. Now may
I offer you my friendship? If I love you,
let me say so. Do not resist me. I appeal
to the spirit of coquetry which tempted you
before you saw me to-night. You are dressed
to please me."

I was thinking what I should say when
he skilfully turned the conversation into
an ordinary channel. He shook off his
dreamy manner, and talked with his old
vivacity. I was charmed a little; an asso-
ciation added to the charm, I fancy. It was
late at night when he took his leave. He
had arranged it all; for a man brought his
carriage to the door and drove him to the
next town, where he had procured it to
come over from the railway.

When I was shut in my room for the
night rage took possession of me. I tore
off my dress, twisted my hair with vehe-
mence, and hurried to bed and tried to go
to sleep; but could not, of course. As when
we press our eyelids together for meditation
or sleep, violet rings and changing rays of

light flash and fade before the darkened
eyeballs, so in the dark unrest of my mind
the past flashed up, and this is what I saw:

The county ball, where Laura and I first
met Redmond, Harry Lothrop, and Maurice.
We were struggling through the crowd of
girls at the dressing-room door, to rejoin
Frank, who was waiting for us. As we
passed out, satisfied with the mutual inspec-
tion of our dresses of white silk, which were
trimmed with bunches of rose-geranium, we
saw a group of strangers close by us, button-
ing their gloves, looking at their boots, and
comparing looks. Laura pushed her fan
against my arm; we looked at each other,
and made signs behind Frank, and were
caught in the act, not only by him, but by
a tall gentleman in the group which she
had signalled me to notice. The shadow of
a smile was travelling over his face as I
caught his eye, but he turned away so suddenly that I had no opportunity for embarrassment. An usher gave us a place near
the band, at the head of the hall.

"Do not be reckless, Laura," I said—"at
least, till the music gives you an excuse."

"You are obliged to me, you know," she
answered, "for directing your attention to

such attractive prey. Being in bonds myself, I can only use my eyes for you; don't
be ungrateful."

The band struck up a crashing polka, and
she and Frank whirled away, with a hundred others. I found a seat and amused myself by contrasting the imperturbable coun-
tenances of the musicians with those of the
dancers. The perfumes the women wore
floated by me. These odors, the rhythmic
motion of the dancers, and the hard, ener-
getic music exhilarated me. The music
ended, and the crowd began to buzz. The
loud, inarticulate speech of a brilliant crowd
is like good wine. As my acquaintances
gathered about me, I began to feel its elec-
tricity, and grew blithe and vivacious. Presently I saw one of the ushers speaking to
Frank, who went down the hall with him.

"Oh, my prophetic soul!" said Laura,
" they are coming."

Frank came back with the three and introduced them. Redmond asked me for the
first quadrille, and Harry Lothrop engaged
Laura. Frank said to me behind his handkerchief, " It's *en règle;* I know where they
came from; their fathers are brave, and their
mothers are virtuous."

The quadrille had not commenced, so I

talked with several persons near; but I felt a constraint, for I knew I was closely observed by the stranger, who was entirely quiet. Curiosity made me impatient for the dance to begin; and when we took our places I was cool enough to examine him. Tall, slender, and swarthy, with a delicate moustache over a pair of thin scarlet lips, penetrating eyes, and a tranquil air. My antipodes in looks, for I was short and fair; my hair was straight and black like his, but my eyes were blue, and my mouth wide and full.

"What an unnaturally pleasant thing a ball-room is!" he said — "before the dust rises and the lights flare, I mean. But nobody ever leaves early; as the freshness vanishes the extravagance deepens. Did you ever notice how much faster the musicians play as it grows late? When we open the windows, the fresh breath of the night increases the delirium within. I have seen the quietest women toss their faded bouquets out of the windows without a thought of making a comparison between the flowers and themselves."

"My poor geraniums!" I said — "what eloquence!"

He laughed, and answered,

"My friend Maurice yonder would have said it twice as well."

We were in the promenade then, and stopped where the said Maurice was fanning himself against the wall.

"May I venture to ask you for a waltz, Miss Denham! it is the next dance on the card," said Maurice; " but of course you are engaged."

I gave him my card, and he began to mark it, when Redmond took it, and placed his own initials against the dance after supper, and the last one on the list. He left me then, and I saw him a moment after talking with Laura.

We passed a gay night. When Laura and I equipped for our ten miles' ride it was four in the morning. Redmond helped Frank to pack us in the carriage, and we rewarded him with a knot of faded leaves.

"This late event," said Laura, with a ministerial air, after we had started, " was a providential one. You, my dear Frank, were at liberty to pursue your favorite pastime of whist, in some remote apartment, without being conscience-torn respecting me. I have danced very well without you, thanks to the strangers. And you, Margaret, have had an unusual opportunity of

2

displaying your latent forces. Three such different men! But let us drive fast. I am in want of the cup of tea which mother will have waiting for me."

We arrived first at my door. As I was going up the steps Laura broke the silence, for neither of us had spoken since her remarks.

"By-the-way, they are coming here to stay awhile. They are anxious for some deep-sea fishing. They'll have it, I think."

I heard Frank's laugh of delight at Laura's wit as the carriage drove off.

It was our last ball that season.

It was late in the spring; and when Redmond came with his two friends and settled at the hotel in our town it was early summer. When I saw them again they came with Laura and Frank to pay me a visit. Laura was already acquainted with them, and asked me if I did not perceive her superiority in the fact.

"Let us arrange," said Harry Lothrop, "some systematic plan of amusement by sea and land. I have a pair of horses, Maurice owns a guitar, and Redmond's boat will be here in a few days. Jones, our landlord, has two horses that are tolerable under the saddle. Let us ride, sail, and be serenaded.

The Lake House, Jones again, is eight miles
distant. This is Monday; shall we go there
on horseback Wednesday?"

Laura looked mournfully at Frank, who
replied to her look,

"You must go; I cannot; I shall go back
to business to-morrow."

I glanced at Redmond; he was contem-
plating a portrait of myself at the age of
fourteen.

"Shall we go?" Laura asked him.

"Nothing, thank you," he answered.

We all laughed, and Harry Lothrop said,

"Redmond, my boy, how fond you are of
pictures!"

Redmond, with an unmoved face, said,

"Don't be absurd about my absent-mind-
edness. What were you saying?" And he
turned to me.

"Do you like our plan," I asked, "of going to the Lake House? There is a deep
pond, a fine wood, a bridge; perch, pickerel,
a one-story inn with a veranda; ham and
eggs, stewed quince, elderberry wine, and
a romantic road to ride over."

"I like it."

Frank opened a discussion on fishing;
Laura and I withdrew, and went to the
window-seat.

"I am light-hearted," I said.

"It is my duty to be melancholy," she replied; "but I shall not mope after Frank has gone."

"'After them the deluge,'" said I. "How long will they stay?"

"'Till they are bored, I fancy."

"Oh, they are going; we must leave our recess."

Frank and she remained; the others bid us good-night.

"I shall not come again till Christmas," he said. "These college chaps will amuse you and make the time pass; they are young—quite suitable companions for you girls. *Vive la bagatelle!*"

He sighed, and, drawing Laura's arm in his, rose to go. She groaned loudly, and he nipped her ears.

"Good-bye, Margaret; let Laura take care of you. There is a deal of wisdom in her."

We shook hands, Laura moaning all the while, and they went home.

Frank and Laura had been engaged three years. He was about thirty, and was still too poor to marry.

Wednesday proved pleasant. We had an early dinner, and our cavalcade started from

Laura's. I rode my small bay horse Folly,
a gift from my absentee brother. His coat
was sleeker than satin; his ears moved perpetually, and his wide nostrils were always
in a quiver. He was not entirely safe, for
now and then he jumped unexpectedly; but
I had ridden him a year without accident,
and felt enough acquainted with him not to
be afraid.

Redmond eyed him.

"You are a bold rider," he said.

"No," I answered—"a careful one. Look
at the bit, and my whip, too. I cut his hind-
legs when he jumps. Observe that I do not
wear a long skirt. I can slip off the saddle,
if need be, without danger."

"That's all very well; but his eyes are
vicious; he will serve you a trick some
day."

"When he does, I'll sell him for a cart-
horse."

Laura and Redmond rode Jones's horses.
Harry Lothrop was mounted on his horse
Black, a superb, thick-maned creature, with
a cluster of white stars on one of his shoulders. Maurice rode a wall-eyed pony. Our
friends Dickenson and Jack Parker drove
two young ladies in a carriage—all the sad-
dle-horses our town could boast of being in

nse. We were in high spirits, and rode fast. I was occupied in watching Folly, who had not been out for several days. At last, tired of tugging at his mouth, I gave him rein, and he flew along. I tucked the edge of my skirt under the saddle-flap, slanted forward, and held the bridle with both hands close to his head. A long sandy reach of road lay before me. I enjoyed Folly's fierce trotting; but, as I expected, the good horse Black was on my track, while the rest of the party were far behind. He soon overtook me. Folly snorted when he heard Black's step. We pulled up, and the two horses began to sidle and prance, and throw up their heads so that we could not indulge in a bit of conversation.

"Brute!" said Harry Lothrop, "if I were sure of getting on again, I would dismount and thrash you awfully."

"Remember Pickwick," I said; "don't do it."

I had hardly spoken when the strap of his cap broke, and it fell from his head to the ground. I laughed, and so did he.

"I can hold your horse while you dismount for it."

I stopped Folly, and he forced Black near enough for me to seize the rein and twist it round my hand; when I had done so Folly turned his head, and was tempted to take Black's mane in his teeth; Black felt it, reared, and came down with his nose in my lap. I could not loose my hands, which confused me, but I saw Harry Lothrop making a great leap. Both horses were running now, and he was lying across the saddle, trying to free my hand. It was over in an instant. He got his seat, and the horses were checked.

"Good God!" he said, "your fingers are crushed."

He pulled off my glove, and turned pale when he saw my purple hand.

"It is nothing," I said.

But I was miserably fatigued, and prayed that the Lake House might come in sight. We were near the wood, which extended to it, and I was wondering if we should ever reach it, when he said:

"You must dismount, and rest under the first tree. We will wait there for the rest of the party to come up."

I did so. Numerous were the inquiries when they reached us. Laura, when she heard the story, declared she now believed in Ellen Pickering. Redmond gave me a searching look, and asked me if the one-story inn had good beds.

"I can take a nap, if necessary," I answered, "in one of Mrs. Sampson's rush-bottomed chairs on the veranda. The croak of the frogs in the pond and the buzz of the blue-bottles shall be my lullaby."

"No matter how, if you will rest," he said, and assisted me to remount.

We rode quietly together the rest of the way. After arriving, we girls went by ourselves into one of Mrs. Sampson's sloping chambers, where there was a low bedstead, and a thick feather-bed covered with a patchwork-quilt of the "Job's Trouble" pattern, a small, dim looking-glass surmounted by a bunch of "sparrow-grass," and an unpainted floor ornamented with home-made rugs which were embroidered with pink flower-pots containing worsted rose-bushes, the stalks, leaves, and flowers all in bright yellow. We hung up our riding-skirts on ancient wooden pegs, for we had worn others underneath them suitable for walking, and then tilted the wooden chairs at a comfortable angle against the wall, put our feet on the rounds, and felt at peace with all mankind.

"Alas!" I said, "it is too early for currant-pies."

"I saw," said one of the girls, "Mrs.

Sampson poking the oven, and a smell of pies was in the air."

"Let us go into the kitchen," exclaimed Laura.

The proposal was agreeable; so we went, and found Mrs. Sampson making plum-cake.

"The pies are green-gooseberry-pies," whispered Laura—"very good, too."

"Miss Denham," shrieked Mrs. Sampson, "you haven't done growing yet.—How's your mother and your grandmother?—Have you had a revival in your church?—I heard of the young men down to Jones's—our minister's wife knows their fathers—first-rate men, she says.—I thought you would be here with them.—'Sampson,' I said this morning, as soon as I dressed, 'do pick some gooseberries. I'll have before sundown twenty pies in this house.' There they are—six gooseberry, six custard, and, though it's late for them, six mince, and two awful great pigeon pies. It's poor trash, I expect; I'm afraid you can't eat it; but it is as good as anybody's, I suppose."

We told her we should devour it all, but must first catch some fish; and we joined the gentlemen on the veranda. A boat was ready for us. Laura, however, refused to go in it. It was too small; it was wet; she wanted to walk on the bridge; she could watch us from that; she wanted some flowers, too. Like many who are not afraid of the ocean, she held ponds and lakes in abhorrence, and fear kept her from going with us. Harry Lothrop offered to stay with her, and take lines to fish from the bridge. She assented, and, after we pushed off, they strolled away.

The lake was as smooth and white as silver beneath the afternoon sun and a windless sky; it was bordered with a mound of green bushes, beyond which stretched deep pine woods. There was no shade, and we soon grew weary. Jack Parker caught all the fish, which flopped about our feet. A little way down, where the lake narrowed, we saw Laura and Harry Lothrop hanging over the bridge.

"They must be interested in conversation," I thought; "he has not lifted his line out of the water once."

Redmond, too, looked over that way often, and at last said,

"We will row up to the bridge, and walk back to the house, if you, Maurice, will take the boat to the little pier again."

"Oh yes," said Maurice.

We came to the bridge, and Laura reached out her hand to me.

"Why, dear," she exclaimed, "you have burnt your face! Why did you," turning to Redmond, "paddle about so long in the hot sun?"

Her words were light enough, but the tone of her voice was savage. Redmond looked surprised; he waved his hand deprecatingly, but said nothing. We went up towards the house, but Laura lingered behind, and did not come in till we were ready to go to supper.

It was past sundown when we rose from the ruins of Mrs. Sampson's pies. We voted not to start for home till the evening was advanced, so that we might enjoy the gloom of the pine wood. We sat on the veranda and heard the sounds of approaching night. The atmosphere was like powdered gold. Swallows fluttered in the air, delaying to drop into their nests, and chirped their evening song. We heard the plunge of the little turtles in the lake, and the noisy crows as they flew home over the distant tree-tops. They grew dark, and the sky deepened slowly into a soft gray. A gentle wind arose, and wafted us the sighs of the pines and their resinous odors. I was happy, but Laura was unaccountably silent.

"What is it, Laura?" I asked in a whisper.

"Nothing Margaret; only it seems to me that we mortals are always riding or fishing, eating or drinking, and that we never get to living. To tell you the truth, the pies were too sour. Come, we must go," she said aloud.

Redmond himself brought Folly from the stable.

"We will ride home together," he said. "My calm nag will suit yours better than Black. Why does your hand tremble?"

He saw my shaking hands as I took the rein; the fact was, my wrists were nearly broken.

"Nothing shall happen to-night, I assure you," he continued, while he tightened Folly's girth.

He contrived to be busy till all the party had disappeared down a turn of the road. As he was mounting his horse, Mrs. Sampson, who was on the steps, whispered to me,

"He's a beautiful young man, now!"

He heard her; he had the ear of a wild animal; he took off his hat to Mrs. Sampson, and we rode slowly away.

As soon as we were in the wood Redmond tied the bridles of the horses together with his handkerchief. It was so dark that my sight could not separate him from his horse. They moved beside me, a vague, black shape. The horses' feet fell without noise in the cool, moist sand. If our companions were near us we could not see them, and we did not hear them. Horses generally keep an even pace when travelling at night—subdued by the darkness, perhaps—and Folly went along without swaying an inch. I dropped the rein on his neck, and took hold of the pommel. My hand fell on Redmond's. Before I could take it away he had clasped it, and touched it with his lips. The movement was so sudden that I half lost my balance, but the horses stepped evenly together. He threw his arm round me, and recoiled from me as if he had received a blow.

"Take up your rein," he said, with a strange voice; "quick! we must ride fast out of this."

I made no reply, for I was trying to untie the handkerchief. The knot was too firm.

"No, no," he said, when he perceived what I was doing, "let it be so."

"Untie it, sir !"

"I will not."

I put my face down between the horses' necks and bit it apart, and thrust it into my bosom.

"Now," I said, "shall we ride fast?"

He shook his rein, and we rode fiercely: past our party, who shouted at us; through the wood; over the brow of the great hill, from whose top we saw the dark, motionless sea; through the long street, and through my father's gateway into the stable-yard, where I leaped from my horse, and, bridle in hand, said "Good-night!" in a loud voice.

Redmond swung his hat and galloped off.

Early next morning Laura sent me a note:

"DEAR MARGARET,—I have an ague, and meanto have it till Sunday night. The pines did it. Did you bring home any needles? On Monday mother will give one of her whist-parties. I shall add a dozen or two of our set; you will come.

"P. S.—What do you think of Mr. Harry Lothrop? Good young man, eh?"

I was glad that Laura had shut herself up for a few days; I dreaded to see her just now. I suffered from an inexplicable feeling of pride and disappointment, and did not care to have her discover it. Laura, like myself, sometimes chose to protect herself against neighborly invasions. We never kept our doors locked in the country; the sending in of a card was an unknown process there. Our acquaintances walked in upon us whenever the whim took them, and it now and then happened to be an inconvenience to us who loved an occasional fit of solitude. I determined to keep in-doors for a few days also. Whenever I was in an unquiet mood I took to industry; so that day I set about arranging my drawers, making over my ribbons, and turning my room upside-down. I rehung all my pictures, and moved my bottles and boxes. Then I mended my stockings, and marked my clothes, which was not a necessary piece of work, as I never left home. I next attacked the parlor—washed all the vases, changed the places of the furniture, and distressed my mother very much. When evening came I brushed my hair a good deal, and looked at my hands, and went to bed early. I could not read then, though I often took books from the shelves, and I would not think.

Sunday came round. The church-bells made me lonesome. I looked out of the window many times that day, and, fixing on the sash one of my father's ship-glasses, swept the sea, and peered at the islands on the other side of the bay, gazing through their openings, beyond which I could see the great dim ocean. Mother came home from church, and said young Maurice was there and inquired about me. He hoped I did not take cold; his friend Redmond had been hoarse ever since our ride, and had passed most of the time in his own room, drumming on the window-pane and whistling dirges. Mother dropped her acute eyes on me while she was telling me this; but I yawned all expression from my face.

As Monday night drew near my numbness of feeling began to pass off; thought came into my brain by plunges. Now I desired, now I hoped. I dressed myself in black silk, and wore a cape of black Chantilly lace. I made my hair as glossy as possible, drew it down on my face, and put round my head a band composed of minute sticks of coral. When all was done I took the candle and held it above my head and surveyed myself in the glass. I was very pale. The pupils of my eyes were dilated, as if I had received some impression that would not pass away. My lips had the redness of youth; their color was deepened by my paleness.

"How handsome I am!" I thought, as I set down the candle.

When I entered Laura's parlor she came towards me and said,

"Artful creature! you know well, this
warm night, that every girl of us would
wear a light dress; so you wore a black
one. How well you understand such matters! You are very clever; your real sensi-
bility adds effect to your cleverness. I see
how it is. Come into this corner. Have
you got a fan? Good gracious! black, with
gold spangles; where *do* you buy your
things? I can tell you now," she continued, "my conversation on the bridge the
other day."

She hesitated, and asked me if I liked her
new muslin. She did look well in it; it was
a white fabric, with red rose-buds scattered
over it. Her delicate face was shadowed by
light brown curls. She was attractive, and
I told her so, and she began again:

"Harry Lothrop said, as he was impaling
the half of a worm,

"'Redmond is a handsome fellow, is he
not?'

"'He is too awfully thin,' I answered, 'but
his eyes are good.'

"He gave me a crafty side-look, like that of
a parrot when he means to bite your finger.

"'Your friend, too,' he added, 'is really
one of the most beautiful girls I ever saw—
a coquette with a heart.'

3

"'Let down your line into the water,' I said.

"He laughed a little laugh. By-the-bye, there is an insidious tenacity about Mr. Harry Lothrop which irritates me; but I like him, for I think he understands women. I feel at ease with him when he is not throwing out his tenacious feelers. Then he said,

"'Redmond is engaged to his cousin. The girl's mother had the charge of him through his boyhood. He is ardently attached to her —the mother, I mean. She is most anxious to call Redmond her son.'

"'Didn't you have a bite?' I said.

"'Well, I think the bait *is* off the hook,' he answered; and then we were silent and pondered the water.

"There are some people I must speak to," and Laura moved away without looking at me.

I opened my fan, but felt chilly. A bustle near me caused me to raise my eyes; Redmond was speaking to a lady. He was in black, too, and very pale. He turned towards me and our eyes met. His expression agitated me so that I unconsciously rose to my feet and warned him off with my fan; but he seemed rooted to the spot. Laura

took care of us both ; she came and stood between us.   I saw her look at him so sweetly
and so mournfully that he understood her
in a moment. He shook his head and walked
abruptly into another room.   Laura went
again from me without giving me a look.
Maurice came up, and I made room for him
beside me.   We talked of the riding-party,
and then of our first meeting at the ball.
He told me that Redmond's boat had arrived,
and what a famous boat it was, and " what
jolly sprees we fellows had, cruising about
with her."   I asked him about his guitar,
and when we might hear him play.   He
grew more chatty, and began to tell me about
his sister when Redmond and Harry Lothrop came over to us, which ended his chat.

The party was like all parties—dull at first,
and brighter as it grew late. The old ladies
played whist in one room, and the younger
part of the company were in another. Champagne was not a prevalent drink in our vil-
lage, but it happened that we had some that
night.

" It may be a sinful beverage," said an old
lady near me, " but it is good."

Redmond opened a bottle for me, we clink-
ed glasses, and drank to an indefinite, silent
wish.

"One more," he asked, "and let us change glasses."

Presently a cloud of delicate warmth spread over my brain, and gave me courage to seek and meet his glance. There must have been an expression of irresolution in my face, for he looked at me inquiringly, and then his own face grew very sad. I felt awkward from my intuition of his opinion of my mood, when he relieved me by saying something about Shelley, a copy of whose poems lay on a table near. From Shelley he went to his boat, and said he hoped to have some pleasant excursions with Laura and myself. He "would go at once and talk with Laura's mother about them." I watched him through the door while he spoke to her. She was in a low chair, and he leaned his face on one hand close to hers. I saw that his natural expression was one of tranquillity and courage. He was not more than twenty-two, but the firmness of the lines about his mouth belied his youth.

"He has a wonderful face," I thought, "and just as wonderful a will."

I felt my own will rise as I looked at him —a will that should make me mistress of myself, powerful enough to contend with and resist or turn to advantage any controlling fate which might come near me.

"Do you feel like singing?" Harry Lothrop inquired. "Do you know Byron's song, 'One struggle more and I am free'?"

"Oh yes," I replied; "it is set to music which suits my voice. I will sing it."

Laura had been playing polkas with great spirit. Since the champagne the old ladies had closed their games of whist for talking, and, as it was nearly time to go, the company was gay. There was laughing and talking when I began, but silence soon after, for the wine made my voice husky and effective. I sang as if deeply moved.

"Lord," I heard Maurice say to Laura as I rose from the piano, "what a girl! She's really tragic."

I caught Harry Lothrop's eye as I passed through the door to go up-stairs; it was burning; I felt as if a hot coal had dropped on me. Maurice ran into the hall and sprang upon the stair-railing to ask me if he might be my escort home. That night he serenaded me. He was a good-hearted, cheerful creature; conceited, as small men are apt to be—conceit answering for size with them—but pleasantly so, and I learned to like him as much as Redmond did.

The summer days were passing. We had all sorts of parties—parties in houses and out-of-doors; we rode and sailed and walked. Laura walked and talked much with Harry Lothrop. We did not often see each other alone, but when we met were more serious and affectionate with each other. We did not speak, except in a general way, of Redmond and Harry Lothrop. I did not avoid Redmond, nor did I seek him. We had many a serious conversation in public, as well as many a gay one; but I had never met him alone since the night we rode through the pines.

He went away for a fortnight. On the day of his return he came to see me. He looked so glad when I entered the room that I could not help feeling a wild thrill. I went up to him, but said nothing. He held out both his hands. I retreated. An angry feeling rushed into my heart.

"No," I said. "Whose hand did you hold last?"

He turned deadly pale.

"That of the woman I am going to marry."

I smiled to hide the trembling of my lips, and offered my hand to him; *but he waved it away*, and fell back on his chair, hurriedly

drawing his handkerchief across his face. I
saw that he was very faint, and stood against
the door, waiting for him to recover.

"More than I have played the woman
and the fool before you."

"Yes."

"I thought so. You seem experienced."

"I am."

"Forgive me," he said, gently; "being
only a man, I think you can. Good God,"
he exclaimed, "what an infernal self-posses-
sion you show!"

"Redmond, is it not time to end this?
The summer has been a long one, has it
not? Long enough for me to have learned
what it is to live. Our positions are re-
versed since we have become acquainted. I
am for the first time forgetting self, and you
for the first time remember self. Redmond,
you are a noble man. You have a steadfast
soul. Do not be shaken. I am not like you;
I am not simple or single-hearted. But I
imitate you. Now come, I beg you will
go."

"Certainly, I will. I have little to say."

August had nearly gone when Maurice
told me they were about to leave. Laura
said we must prepare for retrospection and
the fall sewing.

"Well," I said, "the future looks gloomy, and I must have some new dresses."

Maurice came to see me one morning in a state of excitement to say we were all going to Bird Island to spend the day, dine at the light-house, and sail home by moonlight. Fifteen of the party were going down by the sloop Sapphire, and. Redmond had begged him to ask if Laura and I would go in his boat.

"Do go," said Maurice; "it will be our last excursion together; next week we are off. I am broken-hearted about it. I shall never be so happy again. I have actually whimpered once or twice. You should hear Redmond whistle nowadays. Harry pulls his moustache and laughs his oily laughs, but he is sorry to go, and kicks his clothes about awfully. By-the-way, he is going down in the sloop because Miss Fairfax is going, he says—that tall young lady with crinkled hair; he hates her, and hopes to see her sick. May I come for you in the morning, by ten o'clock? Redmond will be waiting on the wharf."

"Tell Redmond," I answered, "that I will go; and will you ask Harry Lothrop not to engage himself for all the reels to Miss Fairfax?"

He promised to fulfil my message, and
went off in high spirits. I wondered, as
I saw him going down the walk, why it
was that I felt so much more natural and
friendly with him than with either of his
friends. I often talked confidentially to him ;
he knew how I loved my mother, and how I
admired my father, and I told him all about
my brother's business. He also knew what
I liked best to eat and to wear. In return,
he confided his family secrets to me. I knew
his tastes and wishes. There was no common ground where I met Redmond and
Harry.Lothrop. There were too many topics
between Redmond and myself to be avoided
for us to venture upon private or familiar
conversation. Harry Lothrop was an accomplished, fastidious man of the world. I
dreaded boring him, and so I said little. He
was several years older than Redmond, and
possessed more knowledge of men, women,
and books. Redmond had no acquirements,
he knew enough by nature, and I never saw
a person with more fascination of manner
and voice.

The evening before the sailing-party I
had a melancholy-fit. I was restless, and
after dark I put a shawl over my head and
went out to walk. I went up a lonesome

road beyond our house. On one side I heard
the water washing against the shore with
regularity, as if it were breathing. On the
other side were meadows, where there were
cows crunching the grass. A mile farther
was a low wood of oaks, through which ran
a path. I determined to walk through that.
The darkness and sharp breeze which blew
against me from limitless space made me
feel as if I were the only human creature the
elements could find to contend with. I turned down the little path into the deeper darkness of the wood, sat down on a heap of
dead leaves, and began to cry.   .

"Mine is a miserable pride," was my
thought—"that of arming myself with beauty and talent, and going through the world
conquering! Girls are ignorant till they are
disappointed. The only knowledge men proffer us is the knowledge of the heart; it be-
comes us to profit by it. Redmond will
marry that girl. He must, and shall. I will
empty the dust and ashes of my heart as
soon as the fire goes down—that is, I think
so; but I know that I do not know myself.
I have two natures—one that acts, and one
that is acted upon; and I cannot always
separate the one from the other."

Something darkened the opening into the

path. Two persons passed in slowly. I
perceived the odor of violets, and felt that
one of them must be Laura. Waiting till
they passed beyond me, I rose and went
home.

The next morning was cloudy, and the
sea was rough with a high wind; but we
were old sailors, and decided to go on our excursion. The sloop and Redmond's boat left
the wharf at the same time. We expected to
be several hours beating down to Bird Island,
for the wind was ahead. Laura and I, muffled in cloaks, were placed on the thwarts
and neglected; for Redmond and Maurice
were busy with the boat. Laura was silent,
and looked ill. Redmond sat at the helm,
and kept the boat up to the wind, which
drove the hissing spray over us. The sloop
hugged the shore, and did not feel the blast .
as we did. I slid along my seat to be near
Redmond. He saw me coming, and put out
his hand and drew me towards him, looking
so kindly at me that I was melted. Trying
to get at my handkerchief, which was in my
dress-pocket, my cloak flew open, the wind
caught it, and, as I rose to draw it closer, I
nearly fell overboard. Redmond gave a
spring to catch me, and the boat lost her
headway. The sail flapped with a loud bang.

Maurice swore, and we chopped about in the short sea.

"It is your destiny to have a scene where-ever you are," said Laura. "If I did not feel desperate I should be frightened. But these green crawling waves are so opaque, if we fall in we shall not see ourselves drown."

"Courage! the boat is under way," Maurice cried out; "we are nearly there."

And rounding a little point we saw the light-house at last. The sloop anchored a quarter of a mile from the shore, the water being shoal, and Redmond took off her party by instalments.

"What the deuse was the matter with you at one time?" asked Jack Parker. "We saw you were having a sort of convulsion. Our cap'n said you were bold chaps to be trifling with such a top-heavy boat."

"Miss Denham," said Redmond, "thought she could steer the boat as well as I could, and so the boat lost headway."

Harry Lothrop gave Redmond one of his soft smiles, and a vexed look passed over Redmond's face when he saw it.

We had to scramble over a low range of rocks to get to the shore. Redmond anchor-ed his boat by one of them. Bird Island was a famous place for parties. It was a mile in extent. Not a creature was on it except the light-house keeper, his wife, and daughter. The gulls made their nests in its rocky borders; their shrill cries, the incessant dashing of the waves on the ledges, and the creaking of the lantern-in the stone tower were all the sounds the family heard, except when they were invaded by some noisy party like ours. They were glad to see us. The light-house keeper went into the world only when it was necessary to buy stores, or when his wife and daughter wanted to pay a visit to the mainland.

The house was of stone, one story high, with thick walls. The small, deep-set windows and the low ceilings gave the rooms the air of a prison; but there was also an air of security about them; for in looking from the narrow windows one felt that the house was a steadfast ship in the circle of the turbulent sea, whose waves from every point seemed advancing towards it. A pale, coarse grass grew in the sand of the island. It was too feeble to resist the acrid breath of the ocean, so it shuddered perpetually, and bent landward, as if invoking the protection of its step-mother, the solid earth.

"It is perfect," said Redmond to me; "I have been looking for this spot all my life; I am ready to swear that I will never leave it."

We were sitting in a window, facing each other. He looked out towards the west, and presently was lost in thought. He folded his arms tightly across his breast, and his eyes were a hundred miles away. The sound of a fiddle in the long alley which led from the house to the tower broke his reverie.

"We shall be uproarious before we leave," I said; "we always are when we come here."

The fun had already set in. Some of the girls had pinned up their dresses and borrowed aprons from the light-house keeper's wife, and with scorched faces were helping her to make chowder and fry fish. Others were arranging the table, assisted by the young men, who put the dishes in the wrong places. Others were singing in the best room. One or two had brought novels along, and were reading them in corners. It was all merry and pleasant, but I felt quiet. Redmond entered into the spirit of the scene. I had never seen him so gay. He chatted with all the girls, interfering or helping, as the case might be. Maurice brought his guitar, and had a group about him at the foot of the tower stairs. He sang loud, but his voice seemed to fluctuate — now it rang

through the tower, now it was half over-
powered by the roar of the sea. His poetical temperament led him to choose songs in
harmony with the place, not to suit the company—melancholy words set to wild, fitful
chords, which rose and died away according
to the skill of the player. I had gone near
him, for his singing had attracted me.

"You are inspired," I said.

He nodded.

"You never sang so before."

"I feel old to-day," he answered, and he
swept his hands across all the strings ; "my
ditties are done."

After dinner Laura asked me to go out
with her. We slipped away unseen, and
went to the beach, and seated ourselves on
a great rock whose outer side was lapped
by the water. The sun had broken through
the clouds, but shone luridly, giving the sea
a leaden tint. The wind was going down.
We had not been there long when Redmond joined us. He asked us to go round
the island in his boat. Laura declined, and
said she would sit on the rock while we
went, if I chose to go. I did choose to go,
and he brought the boat to the rock. He
hoisted the sail half up the mast, and we
sailed close to the shore. It rose gradually

along the east side of the island, and ter-
minated in a bold ledge which curved into
the sea. We ran inside the curve, where
the water was nearly smooth. Redmond low-
ered the sail, and the boat drifted towards
the ledge slowly. A tongue of land, covered with pale sedge, was on the left side.
Above the ledge, at the right, we could see
the tower of the light-house. Redmond
tied down the helm, and, throwing himself
beside me, leaned his head on his hand, and
looked at me a long time without speaking.
I listened to the water, which plashed faintly against the bows. He covered his face
with his hands. I looked out seaward over
the tongue of land; my heart quaked, like
the grass which grew upon it. At last he
rose, and I saw that he was crying—the
tears rained fast.

"My soul is dying," he said, in a stifled
voice; "I am not more than mortal—I cannot endure it."

I pointed towards the open sea, which
loomed so vague in the distance.

"The future is like that, is it not?
Courage! we must drift through it; we shall
find something."

He stamped his foot on the deck.

"Women always talk so; but men are dif-

ferent. If there is a veil before us we must
tear it away, not sit muffled in its folds,
and speculate on what is behind it. Rise."

I obeyed him. He held me firmly. We
were face to face.

" Look at me."

I did. His eyes were blazing.

" Do you love me ?"

" No."

He placed me on the bench, hoisted the
sail, untied the helm, and we were soon
ploughing round to the spot where we had
left Laura; but she was gone. On the rock
where she was perched a solitary gull, which
flew away with a scream as we approached.

That day was the last that I saw Redmond alone. He was at the party at Laura's house which took place the night before
they left. We did not bid each other adieu.

After the three friends had gone, they sent
us gifts of remembrance. Redmond's keep-
sake was a white fan with forget-me-nots
painted on it. To Laura he sent the pen-
holder which was now mine.

We missed them, and should have felt
their loss had no deep feeling been involved;
for they gave an impetus to our dull country life, and the whole summer had been one
of excitement and pleasure. We settled by

4

degrees into our old habits. At Christmas Frank came. He looked worried and older. He had heard something of Laura's intimacy with Harry Lothrop, and was troubled about it, I know; but I believe Laura was silent on the matter. She was quiet and affectionate towards him during his visit, and he went back consoled.

The winter passed. Spring came and went, and we were deep into the summer when Laura was taken ill. She had had a little cough, which no one except her mother noticed. Her spirits fell, and she failed fast. When I saw her last she had been ill some weeks, and had never felt strong enough to talk as much as she did in that interview. She nerved herself to make the effort, and as she bade me farewell, bade farewell to life also. And now it was all over with her!

I fell asleep at length, and woke late. It seemed as if a year had dropped out of the procession of Time. My heart was still beating with the emotion which stirred it when Redmond and I were together last. Recollection had stung me to the quick. A terrible longing urged me to go and find him. The feeling I had when we were in the boat, face to face, thrilled my fibres again. I saw his gleaming eyes; I could have rushed through the air to meet him. But, alas! exaltation of feeling lasts only a moment; it drops us where it finds us. If it were not so, how easy to be a hero! The dull reaction of the present, like a slow avalanche, crushed and ground me into nothingness.

"Something must happen at last," I thought, "to amuse me, and make time endurable."

What can a woman do when she knows that an epoch of feeling is rounded off, finished, dead? Go back to her story-books, her dress-making, her worsted-work? Shall she attempt to rise to mediocrity on the piano or in drawing, distribute tracts, become secretary of a Dorcas society? or shall she turn her mind to the matter of cultivating another lover at once? Few of us women have courage enough to shoulder out the corpses of what men leave in our hearts. We keep them there, and conceal the ruins in which they lie. We grow cunning and artful in our tricks the longer we practise them. But how we palpitate and shrink and shudder when we are alone in the dark!

After Redmond departed I had locked up my feelings and thrown the key away. The death of Laura, and the awakening of

my recollections, caused by the appearance
of Harry Lothrop, wrenched the door open.
Hitherto I had acted with the bravery of a
girl; I must now behave with the resolution
of a woman. I looked into my heart closely.
No skeleton was there, but the image of a
living man—*Redmond.*

"I love him," I confessed. "To be his
wife and the mother of his children is the
only lot I ever care to choose. He is noble,
handsome, and loyal. But I cannot belong
to him, nor can he ever be mine.

> "'Of love that never found his earthly close
> What sequel?'

What did he do with the remembrance of
me? He scattered it, perhaps, with the ashes of the first cigar he smoked after he went
from me—made a mound of it, maybe, in
honor of Duty. I am as ignorant of him as
if he no longer existed; so this image must
be torn away. I will not burn the lamp of
life before it, but will build up the niche
where it stands into a solid wall."

The ideal happiness of love is so sweet
and powerful that, for a while, adverse in-
fluences only exalt the imagination. When
Laura told me of Redmond's engagement, it
did but change my dream of what might be

into what might have been. It was a mirage which continued while he was present and faded with his departure. Then my heart was locked in the depths of will till circumstances brought it a power of revenge. I think now, if we had spoken freely and truly to each other, I should have suffered less when I saw his friend. We feel better when the funeral of our dearest friend is over and we have returned to the house. There is to be no more preparation, no waiting; the windows may be opened, and the doors set wide; the very dreariness and desolation force our attention towards the living.

"Something will come," I thought; and I determined not to have any more reveries. "Mr. Harry Lothrop is a pleasant riddle; I shall see him soon, or he will write."

It occurred to me then that I had some letters of his already in my possession—those he had written to Laura. I found the ebony box, and, taking from it the sealed package, unfolded the letters one by one, reading them according to their dates. There was a note among them for me from . Laura.

"When you read these letters, Margaret," it said, "you will see that I must have studied the writer of them in vain. You know now that he made me unhappy; not that I was in love with him much, but he stirred depths of feeling which I had no knowledge of, and which between Frank, my betrothed husband, and myself had no existence. But '*le roi s'amuse.*' Perhaps a strong passion will master this man; but I shall never know. Will you?"

I laid the letters back in their place, and felt no very strong desire to learn anything more of the writer. I did not know then how little trouble it would be—my share of making the acquaintance.

It was not many weeks before Mr. Lothrop came again, and rather ostentatiously, so that everybody knew of his visit to me. But he saw none of the friends he had made during his stay the year before. I happened to see him coming, and went to the door to meet him. Almost his first words were:

"Maurice is dead. He went to Florida, took the fever, which killed him, of course. He died only a week after — after Laura. Poor fellow! did he interest you much? I believe he was in love with you, too; but

musical people are never desperate, except
when they play a false note."

"Yes," I answered, "I was fond of him.
His conceit did not trouble me, and he
never fatigued me; he had nothing to conceal. He was a commonplace man; one
liked him when with him, and when away
one had no thought about him."

"I alone am left you," said my visitor,
putting his hat on a chair, and slowly pull-
ing off his gloves, finger by finger.

He had slender, white hands, like a woman's, and they were always in motion. After
he had thrown his gloves into his hat, he
put his finger against his cheek, leaned his
elbow on the arm of his chair, crossed his
legs, and looked at me with a cunning self-
possession. I glanced at his feet; they were
small and well-booted. I looked into his
face; it was not a handsome one, but he
had magnetic eyes of a lightish blue, and a
clever, loose mouth. It is impossible to de-
scribe him — just as impossible as it is for a
man who was born a boor to attain the
bearing of a gentleman; any attempt at it
would prove a bungling matter when compared with the original. He felt my scrutiny, and knew, too, that I had never looked
at him till then.

"Do you sing nowadays?" he asked, tapping with his fingers the keys of the piano behind him.

" Psalms."

"They suit you admirably; but I perceive you attend to your dress still. How effective those velvet bands are! You look older than you did two years ago."

"Two years are enough to age a woman."

"Yes, if she is miserable. Can you be unhappy?" he asked, rising, and taking a seat beside me.

There was a tone of sympathy in his voice which made me shudder, I knew not why. It was neither aversion nor liking; but I dreaded to be thrown into any tumult of feeling. I realized afterwards more fully that it is next to impossible for a passionate woman to receive the sincere addresses of a manly man without feeling some fluctuation of soul. Ignorant spectators call her a coquette for this. Happily, there are teachers among our own sex, women of cold temperaments, able to vindicate themselves from the imputation. They spare themselves great waste of heart and some generous emotion—also remorse and self-accusations regarding the want of propriety and the other ingredients which go to make up a white-muslin heroine.

Harry Lothrop saw that my check was burning, and made a movement towards me. I tossed my head back, and moved down the sofa; he did not follow me, but smiled and mused in his old way.

And so it went on—not once, but many times. He wrote me quiet, persuasive, eloquent letters. By degrees I learned his own history and that of his family, his prospects and his intentions. He was rich. I knew well what position I should have if I were his wife. My beauty would be splendidly set. I was well enough off, but not rich enough to harmonize all things according to my taste. I was proud, and he was refined; if we were married, what better promise of delicacy could be given than that of pride in a woman, refinement in a man? He brought me flowers or books when he came. The flowers were not delicate and inodorous, but magnificent and deep-scented; and the material of the books was stalwart and vigorous. I read his favorite authors with him. He was the first person who ever made any appeal to my intellect. In short, he was educating me for a purpose.

Once he offered me a diamond cross. I refused it, and he never asked me to accept any gift again. His visits were not frequent, and they were short. However great the distance he accomplished to reach me, he stayed only an evening, and then returned. He came and went at night. In time I grew to look upon our connection as an established thing. He made me understand that he loved me, and that he only waited for me to return it; but he did not say so.

I lived an idle life, inhaling the perfume of the flowers he gave me, devouring old literature, the taste for which he had created, and reading and answering his letters. To be sure, other duties were fulfilled. I was an affectionate child to my parents, and a proper acquaintance for my friends. I never lost any sleep now, nor was I troubled with dreams. I lived in the outward; all my restless activity, that constant questioning of the heavens and the earth, had ceased entirely. Five years had passed since I first saw Redmond. I was now twenty-four. The Fates grew tired of the monotony of my life, I suppose, for about this time it changed.

My oldest brother, a bachelor, lived in

New York. He asked me to spend the winter with him; he lived in a quiet hotel, had a suite of rooms, and could make me comfortable, he said. He had just asked somebody to marry him, and that somebody wished to make my acquaintance. I was glad to go. My heart gave a bound at the prospect of change; I was still young enough to dream of the impossible when any chance offered itself to my imagination; so I accepted my brother's invitation with some elation.

I had been in New York a month. One day I was out with my future sister on a shopping raid; with our hands full of little paper parcels, we stopped to look into Goupil's window. There was always a rim of crowd there, so I paid no attention to the jostles we received. We were looking at an engraving of Ary Scheffer's "Françoise de Rimini." "Not the worst hell," muttered a voice behind me which I knew. I started, and pulled Leonora's arm; she turned round, and the fringe of her coat-sleeve caught a button on the overcoat of one of the gentlemen standing together. It was Redmond; the other was his "ancient," Harry Lothrop. Leonora was arrested; I stood still, of course. Redmond had not seen my face, for I turned

it from him; and his head was bent down
to the task of disengaging his button.

> "'Each only as God wills
> Can work; God's puppets, best and worst,
> Are we; there is no last nor first,'"

I thought, and turned my head. He in-
stinctively took off his hat, and then planted
it back on his head firmly, and looked over to
Harry Lothrop, to whom I gave my hand.
He knew me before I saw him, I am convinced; but his dramatic sense kept him silent—perhaps a deeper feeling. There was
an expression of pain in his face which im-
pelled me to take his arm.

"Let us move on, Leonora," I said; "these
are some summer friends of mine," and I
introduced them to her.

My chief feeling was embarrassment,
which was shared by all the party; for Leonora felt that there was something unusual
in the meeting. The door of the hotel seemed
to come round at last, and as we were going
in, Harry Lothrop asked me if he might see
me the next morning.

"Do come," I answered aloud.

We all bowed, and they disappeared.

"What an elegant Indian your tall friend
is!" said Leonora.

"Yes; of the Comanche tribe."

"But he would look better hanging from his horse's mane than he does in a long coat."

"He is spoiled by civilization and white parents. But, Leonora, stay and dine with me in my own room. John will not come home till it is time for the opera. You know we are going. You must make me splendid; you can torture me into style, I know."

She consented, provided I would send a note to her mother, explaining that it was my invitation, and not her old John's, as she irreverently called him. I did so, and she was delighted to stay.

"This is fast," she said; "can't we have champagne and black coffee?"

She fell to rummaging John's closets, and brought out a dusty, Chinese-looking affair, which she put on for a dressing-gown. She found some Chinese straw shoes, and tucked her little feet into them, and then braided her hair in a long tail, and declared she was ready for dinner. Her gayety was refreshing, and I did not wonder at John's admiration. My spirits rose, too, and I astonished Leonora at the table with my chat; she had never seen me except when quiet. I fell into one of those unselfish, unasking moods which are the glory of youth: I felt that the pure heaven of love was in the depths of my being; my soul shone like a star in its atmosphere; my heart throbbed, and I cried softly to it, "Live! live! he is here!" I still chatted with Leonora and made her laugh, and the child for the first time thoroughly liked me. We were finishing our dessert when we heard John's knock. We allowed him to come in for a moment, and gave him some almonds, which he leisurely cracked and ate.

"Somehow, Margaret," he said, "you remind me of those women who enjoy the Indian festival of the funeral pile. I have seen the thing done; you have something of the sort in your mind; be sure to immolate yourself handsomely. Women are the dense."

"Finish your almonds, John," I said, "and go away; we must dress."

He put his hand on my arm, and whispered:

"Smother that light in your eyes, my girl; it is dangerous. And you have lived under your mother's eye all your life! You see what I have done"—indicating Leonora with his eyebrows; "taken a baby on my hands."

"John, John!" I inwardly ejaculated, "you are an idiot."

"She shall never suffer what you suffer; she shall have the benefit of the experience which other women have given me."

"Very likely," I answered; I know we often serve you as pioneers merely."

He gave a sad nod, and I closed the door upon him.

"Put these pins into my hair, Leonora, and tell me, how do you like my new dress?"

"Paris!" she cried.

It was a dove-colored silk with a black velvet stripe through it. I showed her a shawl which John had given me—a pale yellow gauzy fabric with a gold-thread border—and told her to make me up. She produced quite a marvellous effect; for this baby understood the art of dress to perfection. She made my hair into a loose mass, rolling it away from my face; yet it was firmly fastened. Then she shook out the shawl and wrapped me in it, so that my head seemed to be emerging from a pale-tinted cloud. John said I looked outlandish, but Leonora thought otherwise. She begged him for some Indian perfume, and he found an aromatic powder, which he sprinkled inside my gloves and over my shawl.

We found the opera-house crowded. Our seats were near the stage. John sat behind us, so that he might slip out into the lobby occasionally; for the opera was a bore to him. The second act was over; John had left his seat; I was opening and shutting my fan mechanically, half lost in thought, when Leonora, who had been looking at the house with her lorgnette, turned and said:

"Is not that your friend of this morning on the other side, in the second row, leaning against the third pillar? There is a queenish-looking old lady with him. He hasn't spoken to her for a long time, and she continually looks up at him."

I took her glass and discovered Redmond. He looked back at me through another; I made a slight motion with my handkerchief; he dropped his glass into the lap of the lady next him and darted out, and in a moment he was behind me in John's seat.

"Who is with you?" he asked.

"Brother," I answered.

"You intoxicate me with some strange perfume; don't fan it this way."

I quietly passed the fan to Leonora, who now looked back and spoke to him. He talked with her a moment, and then she discreetly resumed her lorgnette.

"What happened for two years after I left
B. ? The last year I know something of."

"Breakfast, dinner, and tea, the ebb and
flow of the tide, and the days of the week."

"Nothing more?" And his voice came
nearer.

"A few trifles."

"They are under lock and key, I suppose?"

"We do not carry relics about with us."

"There is the conductor; I must go.
Turn your face towards me more."

I obeyed him, and our eyes met. His
searching gaze made me shiver.

"I have been married," he said, and his
eyes were unflinching, "and my wife is
dead."

All the lights went down, I thought; I
struck out my arm to find Leonora, who
caught it and pressed it down.

"I must get out," I said; and I walked
up the alley to the door without stumbling.

I knew that I was fainting or dying; as
I had never fainted, I did not know which.
Redmond carried me through the cloak-room
and put me on a sofa.

"I never can speak to him again," I
thought, and then I lost sight of them all.

A terribly sharp pain through my heart

5

ronsed me, and I was in a violent chill.
They had thrown water over my face; my
hair was matted, and the water was drip-
ping from it on my naked shoulders. The
gloves had been ripped from my hands, and
Leonora was wringing my handkerchief.

"The heat made you faint, dear," she
said.

John was walking up and down the room
with a phlegmatic countenance, but he was
fuming.

"My new dress is ruined, John," I said.

"Hang the dress! How do you feel
now ?"

"It is drowned ; and I feel better. Shall
we go home ?"

He went out to order the carriage, and
Leonora whispered to me that she had forgotten Redmond's name.

"No matter," I answered. I could not
have spoken it then.

When John came, Leonora beckoned to
Redmond to introduce himself. John shook
hands with him, gave him an intent look,
and told us the carriage was ready. Redmond followed us, and took leave of us at
the carriage door.

Leonora begged me to stay at her house ;
I refused, for I wished to be alone. John

deposited her with her mother, and we
drove home. He gave me one of his infal-
lible medicines, and told me not to get up
in the morning. But when morning came
I remembered Harry Lothrop was coming,
and made myself ready for him. As human
nature is not quite perfect, I felt unhappy
about him, and rather fond of him, and
thought he possessed some admirable qualities. I never could read the old poets any
more without a pang, unless he were with
me, directing my eye along their pages with
his long white finger! I never should smell
tuberoses again without feeling faint, unless they were his gift!

By the time he came I was in a state of
romantic regret, and in that state many a
woman has answered, " Yes!" He asked
me abruptly if I thought it would be folly
in him to ask me to marry him. The question turned the tide.

" No," I answered, " not folly, for I have
thought many times in the last two years
that I should marry you if you said I must.
But now I believe that it is not best. You
have pursued me patiently; your self-love
made the conquest of me a necessary
pleasure. That was well enough for me,
for you made me feel all the while that, if I

loved you, you were worth possessing. And you are. I liked you. But my feeling for you did not prevent my fainting away at the opera-house last night when Redmond told me that his wife was dead."

"So," he said, " the long-smothered fire has broken out again! Chance does not befriend me. He saw you last night, and yielded. He said yesterday he should not tell you. He asked me about you after we left you, and wished to know if I had seen you much for the last year. I offered him your last letter to read—am I not generous ?—but he refused it.

"'When I see her,' he asked, 'am I at liberty to say what I choose ?'

"On that I could have said, 'No.' Redmond and I had not seen each other since the period of my first visit to you. He has been nursing his wife in the meantime, taking journeys with her, and trying all sorts of cures; and now he seems tied to his aunt and mother-in-law. He was merely passing through the city with her, and this morning they have gone again. Well," after a pause, " there is no need of words between us. I have in my possession a part of you. Beautiful women are like flowers which open their leaves wide enough for their per-

fume to attract wandering bees; the perfume is wasted, though the honey may be
hid."

"Alas, what a lesson this man is giving
me!" I thought.

"Farewell, then," he said. He bit his
lips, and his clinched hands trembled; but
he mastered his emotion. "You must think
of me."

"And see you, too," I answered. "Everything comes round again, if we live long
enough. Dramatic unities are never preserved in life; if they were, how poetical
would all these things be! But Time whirls
us round, showing us our many-sided feelings as carelessly as a child rattles the bits
of glass in his kaleidoscope."

"So be it!" he replied. "Adieu!"

That afternoon I stayed at home, and put
John's room in order, and cleaned the dust
from his Indian idols, and was extremely
busy till he came in. Then I kissed his
whiskers, and told him all my sins, and
cried once or twice during my confession.
He petted me a good deal, and made me eat
twice as much dinner as I wanted; he said
it was good for me, and I obeyed him, for I
felt uncommonly meek that day.

Soon after, Redmond sent me a long

letter. He said he had been, from a boy, under an obligation to his aunt, the mother of his wife. It was a common story, and he would not trouble me with it. He was married soon after Harry Lothrop's first visit to me, at the time they had received the news of Laura's death. How much he had thought of Laura afterwards, while he was watching the fading away of his pale blossom! His aunt had been ill since the death of her daughter, restless, and discontented with every change. He hoped she was now settled among some old friends with whom she might find consolation. In conclusion, he wrote: "My aunt noticed our hasty exit from the opera-house that night, when I was brute enough to nearly kill you. I told her that I loved you. She now feels, after a struggle, that she must let me go. 'Old women have no rights,' she said to me yesterday. Margaret, may I come, and never leave you again?"

My answer may be guessed, for one day he arrived. It was the dusk of a cheery winter day, the time when home wears so bright a look to those who seek it. It was an hour before dinner, and I was waiting for John to come in. The amber evening sky gleamed before the windows, and the fire made a red core of light in the room. John's sandal-wood boxes gave out strange odors in the heat, and the pattern of the Persian rug was just visible. A servant came to the door with a card. I held it to the grate, and the fire lit up his name.

" Show him up-stairs," I said.

I stood in the doorway, and heard his step on every stair. When he came I took him by the hand, and drew him into the room. He was speechless.

" Oh, Redmond, I love you! How long you were away!"

He knelt by me, and put my arms around his neck, and we kissed each other with the first, best kiss of passion.

John came in, and I reached out my hand to him and said, " This is my husband."

"That's comfortable," he answered. " Won't you stay to dinner?"

" Oh yes," replied Redmond ; " this is my hotel."

" I see," said John.

But after dinner they had a long talk together. John sent me to my room, and I was glad to go. I walked up and down, crying, I must say, most of the time, asking forgiveness of myself for my faults, and remembering Laura and Maurice—and then

thinking Redmond was mine with a con-
traction of the heart which threatened to
stifle me.

John took us up to Leonora's that evening; he said he wanted to see if Puss would
be tantalized with the sight of such a
beautiful romantic couple just from fairy-
land, who were now prepared "to live in
peace."

We were married the next day in a church
in a by-street. John was the only witness,
and flourished a large silk handkerchief so
that it had the effect of a triumphal banner.
Redmond put the ring on the wrong finger
—a mistake which the minister kindly
rectified. All I had now for the occasion
was a pair of gloves.

One morning after my marriage, when
Redmond and John were smoking together,
I was turning over some boxes, for I was
packing to go home on a visit to our mother.
I called Redmond to leave his pipe and
come to me.

"You have not seen any of my property.
Look, here it is:

"One bitten handkerchief.

"A fan never used.

"A gold pen-holder.

"A draggled shawl."

"Margaret," he said, taking my chin in his hand and bringing his eyes close to mine, "I am wild with happiness."

"Your pipe has gone out," we heard John say.

IN HONOR BOUND.

BY MISS CAROLINE CHESEBRO.

THE little hamlet called Juniper, lying at the foot of the Granite Hills, had contributed men out of all proportion to the State and country—twenty ministers to the pulpit, a judge to the Court of Appeals, a governor and a bishop to the Northwestern territory. Poor in crops, it had been rich in men. The traditions of the region—for Juniper was yet more a region than a place —were remarkable.

At length, however, came a time when rising generations exhibited all the signs of contented resting on the laurels won, when energy exhibited itself in amassing wealth and in seeking for enjoyment. Farms and stocks looked up as men looked down. There was very little study done by firelight after a long day of labor in the field. The people of Juniper had not yet ceased to worship at the shrines of their ancestors, but the pride kindled by tradition seemed to have lost the element of emulation. There was no more of it. Soul took its ease in Juniper; the sacred fire went out.

In these days of decline Matthew Reardon was born, of a line which had neither part nor lot in this heritage of Juniper glory. His father was not a landed proprietor of even the humblest pretensions, but a blacksmith, who, after roving about with his family of five children from one place to another, finally settled at Juniper, and there remained, because there he was attacked by a disease which put an end to his wanderings. He did not die, but became palsied and purblind; and henceforth his boys and his old woman must get on as best they could.

They exhibited themselves in ways common to people among whom nature is strong. They quarrelled over work, food, clothing, fire; and the weakest of the five—they were all boys—bade fair to be worst off. His mother, perceiving the fact, took the child under her special protection, and thus taught him the great lesson that whatever is desirable in this world may be obtained easily if one have but the wisdom to keep still and use opportunity.

If you ask whether a better character bade fair to be formed in Matthew by this training, and the tact which was thus developed in him, than was fashioned in Abel, the eldest, by his almost desperate use of the weapons with which he had supplied himself when he found that he must take the place of leader in his father's house, I am afraid you must wait some time for an answer.

But without doubt Matthew did make a more agreeable exhibition of himself. He seemed to be gentle, but perhaps was only calculating; he appeared to be generous, possibly was merely timid. Abner Reardon was the fourth son ; Matthew was the second; Michael, the third, had gone to seek his fortune nobody knew where ; Luke was dead since infancy ; and Abel was the eldest.

Abner was the only one of the brothers who seemed to know anything about Matthew, and he was ten years Matthew's junior, and but seven when that wonder of the household died. So it happened quite easily that his imagination, fastening upon the dead, made of him something between human and divine which by no possibility could have found lodgment within Reardon flesh and blood—at least, not at that period of the Reardon history.

Destitute of family record or tradition,
blessed merely with a Saxon common-sense
which controlled well a Celtic imagination,
it is difficult to understand—is it?—his
belief that, had Matthew lived, the world
must have had another notable man out of
Juniper.   *

Abner's destiny was not an unhappy one.
He was born to star - worship — to a devo-
tional impulse towards the station his brother had aimed at.   With the spirit of an-
tagonism strongly developed in him, and
the disposition to appropriate whatever he
wanted, wherever he found it, and to question and decide rights on the unquestion-
able power of the strongest, taking up the
tradition of his brother, he felt within him
the proud purpose that would give back to
his mother what she had really never lost—
comfort a grief which, in the degree he con-
ceived of, she had never borne.   See how
this fiction of an imaginary hero in the house
worked on the life of this lad, and speak
reverently of imagination, the grandest of
gifts to mortals.

Abner believed that Matthew, who was
gentle, had also been brave, and bravely set
to work to acquire a like gentleness.   He
imagined that the born plodder was patient

in the way that *he* must be patient would he win what Mat would certainly have won, and steadily he sought to discipline his rough and fiery wilfulness into order.

As he grew older he saw in his mother a suffering woman who had lost a son by whom, in the midst of savage natures, she had been tenderly loved and served, a son who had been to her as a daughter, and into his heart trickled drops from a divine fountain that made it a well of brightness.

You are in the secret of Abner Reardon's growth. You know how he conquered his dislike for anything like study; how he struggled to win his own approbation; how he stood as a slayer of dragons in the den where he was born. By no miracle was it that a son like Abner loomed up among the Reardons. For the reason that he was nothing that could have been *born* of them, neither the blacksmith nor his wife understood the lad; and in time, as his eyes opened wider, and his brain more clearly perceived, must it not become as evident to himself as to others, and more intelligible to himself than to them, that between them lay a gulf as deep as time, a wall as high as heaven ?

Years passed on, and Abel, of course, married; and as he had already a family to a great degree dependent on him in his father's house, he brought his wife to it, and after that, though there were slight changes, and perhaps a little gain in cheerfulness, things did not, on the whole, go on much better with the Reardons than they had from the beginning.

A young bride, my young lady, who brings no fortune into the home of a poor man, and, alas! not even health, must she not have inexhaustible good nature, faith unlimited, and unquenchable cheerfulness to secure for herself an immovable place in the household affections? Poor Ruth seemed to have all that could be required, for she soon became the centre of the house, and the house was transformed into a home.

Yet it seemed strange to all the neighbors when Ruth Colt went over to the Reardons'. What could have induced her to exchange her father's for the blacksmith's house? Perhaps Abel's bluff kind of manfulness seemed to a delicate girl, who had grown up in a family of girls, full of protecting power. Whatever she expected, whatever she found, it began to appear that Ruth had married Abel and come into the house chiefly that she might instruct Abner how he might find his way out of it.

The twenty ministers, the bishop, and the judge had each and all passed to their high position through college doors, with midnight lamps and text-books in their hands, and Abner had thought of no other way of egress, and had begun to look with doubting gaze towards the future. But Abel's wife came, and made a life-long friend of him by her more than wonderous fairy tale about her uncle in New York, who had begun life as a saddler, and was ending it a millionaire. Perhaps the blacksmith's trade might prove as good a beginning, but the saddler had not got on without learning of some sort. Yes, and had taught school before he set himself up in business! There it all was in a nutshell. The time Abner had given to study had not been lost—the more time he continued to give to it the better—but enterprise also must have its opportunity. Abner boldly took the money he had been saving for college expenses—money he had earned by performing sexton duty in a church five miles away—and, selling the apples which he had dried to a peddler for three cents a pound, he bought tobacco, pipes, cigars, yeast-cakes, matches, soap, and other like light wares, and these he exposed for sale on neat shelves which he put up back of a counter in the little shed adjoining Abel's shop. Many a child has "played store" on the outlay of a larger capital than was expended by the experiment Abner so seriously made. Abel laughed at "the boy;" but there was his own Ruth's story about her uncle, and the Colts had rich relations. Everybody knew it. Abel could not put the testimony of their experiences out of sight.

From time to time, as inquiries were made at the blacksmith's shop for articles of domestic use, the stock on Abner's shelves became larger and more varied, and among the goods were displayed, probably by way of ornament, specimens of quartz and of minerals, which Abner's observing eyes had discovered on his Sunday walks to and from the church where he officiated in his humble capacity.

But Abner was growing older with the months which saw these changes. It took some time to bring about the necessity of enlarged stock, a longer time to collect the specimens and bring them together. Still he never forgot Matthew, and between the books he brought from Juniper Centre Library and the shoeing of horses and the selling of wares he had sufficient occupa-

6

tion. When would the tide rise, though, so as to surge through the inlet, and set the smooth water his bark was moored in in motion.

Sometimes Ruth's younger sister, Abby, came to visit them. She was a lively girl, who had taught school since she was twelve years old—a loving girl, who took no over-burdening thought of the morrow, and was as satisfied with the pleasure of a day as if the promise of eternal duration were in it.

People at the Centre began to say that it would be a pity if another of the Colt girls should be so easily satisfied as to "take" a Reardon, but for all that it was by no means a rare sight on a Sunday morning to see the two walking together on the high-road tow-ards the meeting-house. And, indeed, it seemed quite unlikely that they would make any other disposition of themselves than just this which the gossips suggested with the doubting of sceptics.

One day there came a letter from the Far West to the Colt family, and after it had been duly read and discussed by the house-hold, Abby put it into her pocket and walked over to Abel's, carrying a thought with her which she hardly dared to measure in its length and breadth.

Abner ought to know about the prairies
and the cattle, and how a man might make
a fortune by hardly a turn of the hand if he
would only go far enough away from all he
knew and loved in search of it. That was
the direction towards which the thought
tended. Could she counsel such a step?
What couldn't Abby do for Abner? She
could at least sacrifice herself. He ought to
go from Juniper.

Before she had gone to the house looking
for Ruth, or to the blacksmith's shop seeking Abel — that tall, gaunt, black-browed,
rather dejected-looking man, to whose face
she could bring a kindly smile sooner than
any other being except his wife—Abby went
to speak with Abner, and good reason had
she to be surprised at what she found in his
shop, and near it, for neither at Juniper nor
at Juniper Centre had a like group ever before been seen.

A short, stout, elderly gentleman, whose
head not only, but whose face, seemed to be
covered with beautiful gray hair, a man
who looked capable of coaxing the secrets
out of any kind of nature, stood leaning
against Abner's counter, with every speci-
men that had ornamented the shelves under his loving eyes. He was talking with

Abner. Two young ladies, attired in curious costume, stood near, listening to the conversation, and evidently surprised by the answers the young man was making. One of these girls was Miss Elizabeth Smiles, the professor's daughter. She had all her father's love of Nature, with an equal curiosity concerning the secrets to be disclosed by her, and even more than his disposition to rejoice over every beautiful thing. She was now perceiving in Abner a second Hugh Miller, whom her father would presently in a manner adopt, and by a rapid mental process peculiar to herself, by which she decided on the destiny of all whom she met, Miss Elizabeth set Abner forward on the path of discovery, and made him a ruler in the field of modern science. Whether Abner's powerful eyes, his deliberateness of speech, or the rugged kind of splendor which was revealed in his face when he smiled, helped her in forming her conclusions, I do not know, but my guess in the matter is worth as much, perhaps, as another person's, and I guess she was so assisted. Miss Elizabeth held the lamp of Aladdin in her hand.

Abel was busy shoeing a horse, and talking at the same time with the professor's wife about a cut the animal had received from a sharp stone, just above the ankle, which had lamed him somewhat. A group of three girls stood near, watching the operation as gravely as though they were taking a lesson in a branch of horsemanship new to them. The horses on which the party had been mounted were fastened to the trees close by, and it was evident that the riders had depended on the animals they might chance to find on their journey to take them from place to place.

Nobody noticed Abby, though Abner, she knew, had seen her as she came around the corner; but he made no sign to show that he had. She did not, for that reason, retire to the house. Nobody noticed her, and there was too much to be seen—the individuals of the party, the beauty of some of the faces, the oddity of the attire, excited her curiosity; their voices enchanted her. When at last they had mounted their steeds and rode away, she still lingered within sight and sound of what was going on.

Abner came from behind the counter as the gentleman turned from it, and repeated his promise that he would be ready to go with him the next morning at any time he might call for him, and then stood looking after them as they slowly rode away towards the Juniper Inn, and would not have ventured to offer his assistance when the ladies were mounting the steeds had he not been asked to hold a rein or a stirrup, and to pick up a riding-whip.

When he returned to his shop he saw Abby sitting on the trunk of a tree a little way up the hill-side. "There!" he said, "I know you would be coming. What do you think?"

"I think volumes," said she.

"But what have you there? A letter?"

"Something worth your reading."

"Read it to me. Will you?" Claiming service, rebuking his claim in the same breath—that was Abner.

Abby read the letter. He leaned over the counter, his face supported between his two hands, his eyes glowing, and listened.

A bright fire blazed on the hearth of the Juniper Inn; for though the month was June, night brought not rarely a more than chilling breeze through the valley of the Granite Hills.

Surrounded by his wife and the five girls, all his summer pupils, as he called them, because he loved his vocation so well, sat Pro-

fessor Smiles, happy in his element. Cau-
tion, who had mild suggestions to make to
Enthusiasm now and then, when it appeared probable that the latter might entice the
girls too fast and too far, was now counsel-
ling him. Fortunate were the girls to have
for their guide a man on culture bent, and
intent, too, on proving that the natural sci-
ences offered the best aids to mental discipline anywhere to be found.

To this select audience around the fire he
repeated the story which he had somewhere
heard of the Juniper heroes, the twenty ministers, the bishop, and the judge.

Elizabeth would have said, but for her
conviction that the girls would laugh if she
said it, "And there's another hero preparing
to graduate from the blacksmith shop."

True to the purpose with which he had
set out on his tour, the professor had been
his own guide so far, but he had begun to
see that he was not getting his share of the
rest which the vacation should give him, nor
securing exactly the results he had defined
to himself before he set out. A male companion who should serve other purposes
than those of a servant merely would great-
ly lighten his cares. He had been thinking
of the available young men in the Polytech-

nic School and the School of Mines, but
when he took into consideration the party
to whom such student must be attendant,
he found that there was no one at liberty
whom he would call to his aid. Had he now
and here, in this out-of-the-way place, found
the very person whom he needed ? It would
tally with many of Professor Smiles's experiences should he find that this was so. He
was always expecting the best things, and
generally finding them. After the young
people and his wife had left him, while he
sat dreaming before the ashen embers, the
professor recalled and dwelt upon the intelligent face of the possible heir of all the
Juniper greatness, until he became almost
impatient of the hours which must pass before the morning walk among the hills which
would show him whether he had found here
a guide.

"Something worth the reading," said Abby, as she looked up from her letter.

Abner drew the sheet of paper towards
him without speaking, and read it slowly
for himself.

"That is the place for making money,"
said he at length, folding the letter and giving it back to her.

Abby was eloquent in answer, more so by her voice and glance than by her words even.

"You understand it, don't you? You buy the cattle, and brand them with your name, and then let them run. There is no feeding. They feed themselves. The prairies make a pretty wide field. All you have to do when you want to sell is to catch them, and they are all ready."

"Yes," said Abner, "if they don't all get the cattle disease and die off, so when you want 'em they can't be found."

"I never thought of that," said Abby. "There's always something starting up you don't expect."

"Yes," said Abner; but he looked quickly at Abby, as if he would encourage her by some cheerful words if she really needed to hear them. Then he thought how quickly she had come over to Juniper to let them know about her cousin's good-fortune—in prospect.

"I'd rather go to Kansas," said he. "But if I went, I must go alone. I wouldn't ask anybody to go with me."

"I suppose not," she answered. · "Why should you—unless you could find somebody who had money."

"You know what I mean, Abby," he said, slowly and so gravely that she blushed; but she rallied.

"It wouldn't be as handy boarding round in wigwams as it is in New Hampshire, I expect."

Abner laughed now.

"If a girl should go out there with me she would have a rough time of it. She would have to board in her own cabin week in and week out, and no neighbors, like enough. That would be lonesome. But, West or East, it's all the same, so one is satisfied."

"Who is satisfied?" asked Abby. "That's the reason West or East isn't all the same to anybody. You are satisfied, thinking you will bring things around to your liking some time. But you're not satisfied to have them stay as they are. If you are, I'm not."

Abner's eyes brightened. "You have hit the nail on the head," said he. "If you would go with me, I would be a fool to leave you behind."

There seemed to be nothing to say to that—at least, Abby said nothing directly in response; but she spoke directly to the point when she took from her pocket a little book, and said:

" Little Sammy Newton lent me the *Tourist's Guide*—here it is. Kansas is a long way off. But you see they have marked out a railroad, and there—there are those great wide gardens, the prairies." Ah, now it was the pioneer that spoke, that heroic heart whose destiny it is to make our future. She pointed with rather tremulous finger to the section marked Kansas.

Abner took the book from her—the little paper-covered book, with its great map which folded into compass of insignificant proportions—book which thousands of eyes, old and young, have scanned as closely, as believingly, as ever childhood scanned the wonder-books of fable—book that will be studied more and more intently by succeeding generations. Long he studied it in the twilight, while lines and names were becoming obscure. At last he folded it, and gave it back to Abby.

" It would be all work out there," he said; " but the chances are first-rate. If I should make up my mind to go, Abby, would you go with me ?"

She did not answer instantly, and he added,

" It wouldn't be right to ask it ?"

" Why wouldn't it ?" said she, quickly. " What difference would it make to me ?"

"Could we make a home there?"

"Could we anywhere?"

"If we couldn't, I don't want any."

"Same here," she said, in a playful, cheerful tone; but there were tears in her eyes. "Let me know half an hour before you are ready to start. You shall have your fortune if I can help you to it."

Abner understood her. And he knew that he had not won Abby quite as easily as he seemed to have done. But he was far enough from guessing all her thoughts. What man, what woman, in a like moment has guessed all the other's thoughts?

"We should risk all we have," said he, "and you would be the loser, if either of us, Abby."

"I have all to gain, and nothing to lose," she said.

"Well, then, I think before long we will go and look up your cousin."

Hand in hand they walked back to the house, and then Caleb's letter was talked over by Abby and Ruth, and the sisters recalled the day when the orphan boy left their father's house for the West with only his two hands for his stock in trade, and now he had his flocks and his herds, and

seemed sure of Fortune's favor. Abel listened to it all, and said, finally :

"If you only go fur enough, and make up
your mind what you want before you start,
and can put up with nothin', you are all
right. I don't want one o' them red dev-
ils carrying round *my* top-knot in his
pocket."

While they talked and argued, Abner
walked out of the house, and made no haste
to return. A great fire was slowly making
its way through his life's secret chamber.
The material was heavy—ignited with difficulty ; but it had been kindled, and it
would be long before the flame went out.

He went to his shop, restored the minerals to their places on the shelves again, and
looked around him, not with the eyes of a
pleased proprietor, but with the observa-
tion of a critic who has discovered a standard more exacting than he has known before.

His aspect as he stood there reflecting on
the Kansas prospect, and on the party whom
he was to escort in the morning to Hopper's
Glen, ten miles distant, might not have led
a stranger to suspect what had passed between a spirited young woman and himself
during that past hour. Yet he had not been

able to dwell upon the fact that was now
established with regard to their future as he
sat in the house. He required all out-doors,
the heavens above and the stars, the free
air and the hills, for the tabernacle of that
fact. The doubt he had long entertained
whether this bright-minded Abby would
ever consent to share his slow fortunes—for
he had not seen without perceiving the skilful hand with which she brought order out
of disorder wherever she went, and how rich
she was in suggestion when other people
seemed to be at their wits' end — had cost
him much disquiet, and now it was removed!
He could not but be amazed. No place short
of Kansas seemed to offer him a field large
enough and conditions generous enough for
the enterprise he must engage in, with Abby
for a partner.

So it was that he could not sit quietly in
the house thinking of these things, and hear
Abel talk about the lack of timber in Kansas
and the prairie fires, the cattle disease, and
the Indians. How should he suspect that
Abel in this talk was merely trying to reason himself into content with his own small
chance at fortune, and curbing his restive
spirit to do the plodding work of duty, ex-
pounding, in his way, the doctrine of com-

pensation, which he had once heard preached
by New England's high-priest ?

It was full ten miles to Hopper's Glen, and
as the way was none of the smoothest, the
professor had decided to go on foot, and,
quite contrary to expectation, his wife and
the five girls decided to accompany him,
and made such a scornful outcry, when he
had thrown ten miles of difficulty in their
way, that he was quite ready to yield; and
having ascertained that the tourists were
prepared in advance for climbing rocky hill-
sides, and for crossing, if need be, unbridged
streams and swamp lands, all set forth.

Going or returning, the young people
never lost sight of the professor or their
guide. They rested by the way-side under
forest trees, examining the floral specimens
gathered as they went; with their small
hammers they tapped a cheerful tune on the
venerable rocks, and they enriched themselves with the crystals which seemed to be-
seech of them release from the place of their
captivity. They made themselves at home
in Nature's grounds, and manifestly were
her dearly beloved children.

Abner thought of Matthew on that excursion, and blushed to think how high he had

supposed his own aims to have been, how
low they really were. The professor mani-
fested no little desire to be taught concerning the region; and Abner could tell him
the "lay of the land," and the formation of
the rocky region within a radius of fifty
miles, as well as if he had studied a treatise
on the subject. He had once accompanied
an engineer, who went seeking the most
direct line for a railway across the State,
and in that tour Abner had learned to use
his eyes. The rocks, trees, streams, had
taken their place in his memory, and whatever information that was desired concerning them he could give. The professor was
not so much surprised as pleased. He knew
how in that barren land, side by side with
the need which demanded labor of the
hands, fair culture throve; and had Abner
been ten times as well versed in book-
knowledge as he was, it would not have
astonished him.

But those girls, would they not have been
astonished had Abby also been of the party?
Let them try conjugating Latin verbs with
her, or quoting from Vergil, or singing with
the birds, or dishing up a good meal under
unpropitious circumstances! I wish Abby
had been of that company. Would she have

had, as Abner had, an at first overwhelming sense of the distance that lay between her and her company? Perhaps, and probably on her own behalf; but she would have been astonished and indignant that Abner shared the humiliation.

Poor fellow! true to his inspiration, he said, "Mat would not have felt it, because it wouldn't have existed." But, as one moment swiftly followed another, the ideal Mat supplied Abner with reasons why he should stand erect in this company, and with modest self-respect he finally stood erect. Oh, Matthew Reardon, if you saw your work, were not you amazed thereat? Nevertheless, Hail to every veiled prophet, thought of whom has nourished in human hearts the passion of worship!

The next day after this excursion to the Glen, which far exceeded in its wonderful beauty anything that had been imagined by the most fancy-free of the little party, Professor Smiles went down to Abner's shop, and proposed that he should join him and the ladies as a guide on their projected trip across the State to the White Hills.

They expected, he said, to be absent from home a month or six weeks longer; and, besides expenses, fair wages would be allowed.

7

The professor dwelt briefly on the advantages the young man might derive from the trip, and gave him a day to decide.

Here was a great opportunity. Should Abner reject it, think lightly of it, grind on with his feeble hand Fortune's grist, while here was the great windmill, with all the winds of heaven waiting to fill the sails? It depended on how he looked at the chance. The professor had explained it well. The lad was no fool; he could not see far into the future, but he could see with tolerable eyes the present. One day with this party had given him a hundred new ideas. Perhaps Abby could look after the shop; she intended to spend her vacation, now at hand, with Ruth. Why did he say to himself instantly, rather than allow her to perform such service, he would give his wares over to moth, rust, and mildew? Let it not be supposed that had Abner been required to give his answer to the professor within an hour he could not have given it. There was, in reality, no hesitation in his mind, merely the shadows of a few doubts which were hovering around, but would never come boldly into sight.

In the female mind of the family, however, another view was taken of this oppor-

tunity than Abner took. Abel's wife, who
had been thinking with increasing enthusiasm, not to say longing, of the cattle on
those plains, where the way to fortune was
made easy, asked—and no wonder—"Will
tramping over the hills be the same, or better, than getting ready for Kansas? Time
is worth something;" while the mother of
sainted Matthew was troubled about the apple crop, which should have instant attention if Abner expected to send to market his
hundred bushels of dried fruit, as he did last
year. It is indeed a grave matter to let go
the hold on certainty— such chasing of
chimeras as the appalled human heart has
seen since the beginning!

"Maybe not," Abner said to Ruth. "I
must take my chance, though; and, anyway,
there'll be room for me in Kansas after that.
It seems to me as if a door had opened, and
I must go in." To his mother he said, "The
apple business is very well in its way, but I
think I see a short-cut to college." And he
said the same thing to Abby, though in other
words; and she answered, with the understanding and the heart:

"Go with 'em, Abner. As you say, Kansas
is as likely to stand fast as anything. You
can take your chance there any time."

Her encouraging word seemed to decide him. He acknowledged to himself that it did—so it was all one. Abby was associated with his decision—for better, for worse. Doubtless he would have gone without her encouragement, but it was in accordance with all that favored his going out that she should see, as he did, that there was a chance not to be made light of. No matter whether all or half he expected, or nothing, came of the "tramping," Abby would never go back of her counsel and lament it. She did not belong to the stoics, who never repent, but had the steady brain of a Juniper girl, and counselled according to her light, and took the consequences bravely. I would like to discourse on Abby, but I resist the temptation.

The next day saw Abner Reardon going out of Juniper, not to return that season, nor for many another.

The professor liked the young man at the outset, and as they proceeded on their journey, day after day, he liked him more and more, and at length, when the right moment had come, he proposed that he should go back with him to town as his assistant, offering him as compensation a home in his own house and a collegiate course.

The proposal startled Abner. He wrote
home to Abby. What did Abby answer?
"You and I are just such idiots that we can
not see that New England is your trump
card, and not Kansas." So Abner went back
with the professor to Boston; and is there
need that I should show that the gentleman
had secured an invaluable assistant? Anybody can tell how it was that he proved
himself invaluable who considers the discipline to which Abner had subjected himself since he began to think. He was master of himself in many directions: more
methodical, more painstaking and exact, than
any other student in college; and so thoroughly did he understand the truest way of
getting on that he yielded only at rare intervals to the make-shifts of brilliant lazi-
ness. I am compelled in all seriousness to
say of him, in commendation, what one can
hardly suggest now in reference to thinker
or worker without exciting critical suspi-
cion or pathetic commiseration—that he was
"conscientious" in his work.

There seemed to be reason sufficient why
he should not return to Juniper invariably
at holiday seasons. He had, in fact, few
holidays that were his own for leisure. His
vacations were spent chiefly in journeys

with or for Professor Smiles. He made the
tour of libraries and laboratories; his hands
seemed to be always full of notes in short-
hand; and time sped so fast he had had
hardly opportunity for indulging in a regretful thought concerning Juniper. And
when now and then at rare intervals he did
go back to the silent hill country, do you
think it was all the same as if during his
absence he had worked in a less absorbed
way? How is it with those who plunge
into trade or politics to win the glory or
the gold wherewith they will go back to
adorn the home and secure the ideal? Do
they find the old home where they left it?
Is it forever to remain what it was when
the heart loved it best? Is the ideal there?
Abby was there, that good girl who loved
him; and his poor old mother; sickly Ruth;
the little house full of children; Abel, growing gray and wrinkled; the paralytic father; hills that looked not so high as once;
a blacksmith's shop, into which no thought,
apparently, beyond that of rudest labor had
ever entered. Envy not the youth those
visits home. Twice he returned thither,
and the professor, who watched him nar-
rowly, inspecting him on his return the second time, said to himself, "This will never

do. He must stay with me till he has his
diploma, or he will lose all heart and courage." The professor had himself known
the early privation, the humble home, the
dismay awaiting awakened intelligence that
has not yet compassed the all of human experience. He understood what he perceived in Abner when he came back from
these visits, and therefore determined that
they should not be repeated. " Get thee out
of thine own country," " Forget thy people
and thy father's house," he would have said
in so many words had he not had the
knowledge of a more excellent way.

Abner began to be talked about in college circles, and to appear now and then in
social gatherings. Wise ones said that he
was made of " the right stuff," and to speak
of him as a young man of great promise.
Elderly ladies took notice of him ; and there
was one young lady—I need not say the
professor's daughter Elizabeth, who studied
botany, chemistry, and mineralogy with
him—a young lady in whom scientific pre-
dilections were as the vital spark—who
sometimes congratulated herself on the
summer trip which had discovered Abner.
This young lady ! Must it not have been a
pleasant thing for a young working-man like

Abner, whose hands and whose thoughts found so constantly noble occupation, to have for a companion one who understood his successes because she understood so well the obstacles he had overcome in winning them? Could a comparison between his old home and his present abode suggest itself, and not suggest also a train of thought which might lead—who would dare to predict, who could avoid predicting, whither?

And this companion was a handsome girl, quick-witted, gay-hearted, sweet-tempered, capable of hard study and of deep thought, and the daughter of the man who had proved his best friend, his more than father. Poor Abby! But then, after all, even the great wall of China could not secure from the nineteenth century the foredoomed Celestials. And all things must take their chances.

In writing to Abby one day Abner perceived a reluctance which was perhaps not quite new, but which was more intelligible than it had been before. It occasioned a peculiar movement of his pen, and its suspension in the air. It seemed unlikely that he would add another word. And yet he did add many. He deliberately entered on an elaborate description of the social aspect

of his life in the city, and it was almost as
if he thought that by doing this his dear
girl might possibly be led to see with her
own eyes more than he could say—how unlike Juniper life this life he was living was,
and how improbable it was that Juniper, or
anybody in Juniper would ever have in him
the man anticipated. It became after that
his desire to find out how many of all Juniper's great men had gone back to Juniper
for a wife. How strange it was that, after
months and months of waiting, he had
found courage to speak to Abby the very
night when the professor came to Juniper!

Looking at the relations he sustained to-
ward Abby with the unpoetic eyes of common-sense, it must at once be seen that for
Abner to have cherished at this time any
great enthusiasm in view of those relations
would argue a very remarkable youth indeed. Do you, my reader, happen to know
one such elect of invincibles? Of stanch
fidelity he might be capable, but consider
how society dazzles the gray-beards, and
then think of this lad. The well-dressed
woman of the world wills not to be rudely
ignored by the rustic genius. Soft hair,
sweet eyes, sweet voices, perfumes, gar-
ments, graces, know you not all your worth?

Correspondence between Juniper and Boston did not rival telegrams. Four-footed beasts could do all its work acceptably. No need of the birds of the air.

One day Abner received a letter from Abby, saying that Abel's wife had died, and that she was staying with the family. There was great need of a strong-handed woman in the house, and poor Abel, she knew not what would become of him. And then the children, the poor little motherless children, that were to live and grow up in this hard world!

Abner read it, and he felt not a little grieved, thinking of poor Ruth. But the letter came at a time when he was more than usually occupied with laboratory and class work, and when his eyes happened to fall on it several hours after he had received it, he was chiefly shocked to find how little impression the death even of this woman, whom he had once thought of as a great family blessing, had made upon him.

When his hurry was over he deliberately sat down to think upon all these entanglements and snares which beset him, and one result of his thinking was that he told Elizabeth about Abby and the Kansas cattle plan, which had been unexpectedly de-

feated by the coming of her father and the
party by whom he was carried out of Juniper. Consider his condition. Could he
have told her with any other hope than
that by so doing he would be thrown upon
his honor, and stand committed to noblest
behavior before the professor's daughter,
that noblest woman in the world? And yet
he had been thinking, " Poor Abel! what
will become of him, with all that load on
him? Abby was always fond of his children. He will be obliged to marry again.
What a mother she would prove to those
motherless little ones! No other man than
Abel—but—"

A curious train of thought for a young
lover to take up and seriously entertain,
and not for a day only. A month, six weeks
passed, six months, and the thought was
not yet worn threadbare and dismissed.
One day Abner went to the professor and
said : "Do not think me foolish. I know
exactly how things stand. I shall have my
diploma within a fortnight, if ever, and
there's not a little work to be done ; but I
must go home. I can't study. I can't fix
my mind on anything. They need me there
to settle things. We have met with a loss.
They do not say it outright, but I know I

can be of great service to all, and there is no use of my trying to accomplish anything here as I am now."

The professor looked surprised, of course. It was not the report of himself he could have expected of Abner, his model of self-discipline, but he said: "If you must go, you must; but I should be sorry if anything hindered your going abroad with us after Commencement, my son."

When Abner looked at Elizabeth, who was in the room preparing certain botanical specimens for her father's class, she, absorbed in her work, felt that he was looking at her, and, half lifting her eyes, said:

"Who knows what the young lady will say? Perhaps she can go too."

What did she mean by that? As kindly as she said? Was it probable that she would be so ill-bred and so cruel as to smite and humiliate him by the suggestion of an impossibility, which, had it been a possibility, would still perhaps have pleased him so little?

The professor looked from his daughter to Abner, as if about to exclaim, "How's that?" but he did not say it.

Having found the way so clear to Juniper, Abner advanced. He took it without

reluctance—but with gladness? Yes, but
gladness may have little joy. When the
sense of honor must be appealed to in behalf of love, how is it with love? Abner
packed his worldly goods in a portmanteau,
and went to Juniper to say to Abby what
he could not write. He would know whether
it must be said the instant he looked at her.
If either of them had made a mistake choos-
ing for life and life's happiness, best for life,
liberty, and sacred honor that they should
know it before the further and more fatal
mistake had been made. He believed that
the first mistake was not to be denied. He
must explain things to Abby, must talk with
her face to face, and after that they would
always be friends.

So he left the city, and went by the
crowded routes of travel homeward till he
came within fifty miles of Juniper, then by
stage; and at last, on foot, he approached
the blacksmith's shop and the house of
Reardon.

The door of the old brown house stood
open as he approached. How every vine
and shrub and tree in the neighborhood had
grown during those two years which had
not been broken by return! The lilac bushes
were as a wall shielding the house from the

road, and gave to the place an aspect of se-
clusion, though the blacksmith's shop was
so close at hand. The old trees looked
older, the old house more humble. A little
yellow-haired girl was swinging on the gate
—Abel's motherless girl, he knew—with a
flower in her hand. Ruth stood there when
he went away, with a smile on her face and
tears in her kind eyes, and wished him well.
Where was she now ? Could she from any
near or far distance look upon him as he
came ?

He spoke to the little girl. But she had
forgotten him, and when he looked at her
with such scrutiny in his eyes, she jumped
down from the gate and ran into the house.
He made no haste to follow her, but stood
looking around him ; and so, presently, a
voice quite near said to him :

"You might come in, perhaps."

Then he saw Abby standing in the gateway looking at him with a gaze every whit
as terrifying as he had bestowed just now
upon the child, but merely because they
were Abby's own eyes that looked, calm,
steady, tender.

Here, then, was Abel's wife and the
mother of Ruth's motherless children. He
ventured a question, like one half wakened

from sleep and from nightmare. Yet he
had not come home to play with words.

"Are you ready for Kansas?" said he.

"Are you?" she asked in turn.

"We will talk about that," he answered.
"Where's mother?"

Was it mere honor that had spoken?
Must he now shame himself by his midnight
reflections on duty, after he had heard from
Abel and his mother how Abby had been as
the mother of the household since poor
Ruth's death, even as Abner and as Abner's
wife, the mother and the servant of all?

Possibly he had need to test himself still
further in order to discover whether he was
in honor bound. Possibly Abby, aware of
what she did, supplied the test; but I think
not. I think it was rather the result of sad
and solemn thinking that made her say to
him, next day, when she had made for herself an opportunity:

"Abner, the neighbors say I ought to
marry Abel."

"They know what your duty is, I dare
say," he answered, with a glow on his face
kindled by what fire, let us hope, she would
never suspect.

"But I am thinking the same thing."

"Abel too, I dare say."

"I don't know. But—poor Abel!"

"You expect me to give you away—is that it? To-day, then, for I must go back to-morrow."

"I expect your consent," she said, gravely, so much absorbed by what she had to say and by what she was saying that she seemed to pay no heed to what was evidently enough passing within his mind, who had so unexpectedly found the door of deliverance opening. "Abel must marry. There are all those children—who can take care of them as well? And the old people? As to you—" She did not look at him.

"As to me," he said, turning his back suddenly on the 'door of which I have spoken, and expressing himself with a directness which must have amazed him, "if I am not worth your taking, let it be as you have said."

"I have set my common-sense at work," said she. "I have thought a great deal about it. Boston isn't like Juniper. It is inhabited by another kind of people."

"It is indeed," said he.

"Your kind—not mine."

"I deny that."

"Well, you can find your kind there."

"When I have found already what I want, and it is mine!"

"Don't think of that, Abner," she said, quickly. "That belonged to the old time. Since then everything is changed. I have often thought it never could have happened if I hadn't come over that night with Cousin Caleb's letter." She was sufficiently in earnest.

"Then you have learned to love Abel— and it was a mistake about me," said Abner, slowly.

"I have learned many things since you went away."

How did it happen that a little later in the day Abner was calling on all that was within him to prove to Abby that a diploma wasn't worth the having if it took him away from her again?

"So far as I can see," she said, "you are in honor bound to the professor. No Kansas for us yet." Where had she learned those words which had haunted and tormented him so long? And did he tell her then, by way of warning, that Miss Elizabeth was there in the place to which she would return him? Not he. He had forgotten Miss Elizabeth. It was, in fact, Abby's talk that sent Abner the next day back to town, and

8

that constrained him to remain there until he should have rendered some invaluable service to Professor Smiles. But who does not behold on the far Kansas plains a thousand cattle bearing A. R.'s brand ?

What did Abner see in the eyes of Miss Elizabeth when he went back ? Bountiful loving-kindness. And—no more ? No more that he could interpret.

"I should have expected the heavens to fall as soon as to hear that you did not know your own heart and mind, Abner. I never could have forgiven you if you had not seen how you were in honor bound."

"Ah!" said he; "but that was not it, Miss Elizabeth. Though, perhaps, I thought it was."

"I know it," said she.

Thank God for every creature who in the Father's House makes himself a zealous custodian of the sacred ideals!

AN·ISLANDER.

BY MISS MARGARET CROSBY.

I.

AT four o'clock on a September afternoon Vestal Street, Nantucket, is curiously quiet. The square white houses stand on either side of the sandy road. The lowering sunlight is beginning to cast a gray shadow across its glaring whiteness. The houses have no outside shutters, and the closed inside blinds, of solid wood painted white, have a sightless expression. Beyond, in Lily Street and in the lower part of the town, many of the houses have a railed platform on the roof, called the "walk," where the Nantucket wives were wont, in former days, to watch longingly the outward or homeward bound sails; but in Vestal Street the houses have not this dignity. From their upper windows is seen the old windmill, on its green mound, and

the moor, undulating unbrokenly for three
miles until the sea is reached.

On such an afternoon in one of these
houses an elderly man and woman sat in the
living-room talking together. Both were
seated in black wooden rocking-chairs; and
as these two persons talked they rocked,
the creaking of the chairs keeping up a
groaning accompaniment to their conversation.

"So Eunice wouldn't go to the Continent
with Mrs. Lane?" said the old man. "Well,
Mrs. Adams, I always said she was one of
the elect."

He was small and thin; his face was
smooth-shaven, all but a fringe of white
beard that started close to his ears and ran
around under his chin. The same fringe
grew low down on his bald head and waved
on the collar of his blue flannel coat. His
face, thus left exposed, had an expression of
innocent curiosity and kindliness.

At one of the windows a shutter was
open, and a square of blue mosquito-netting
in a frame fitted into the casements and
kept the flies out. Mrs. Adams sat by this
window making a patch-work quilt, and
rocking gently as she sewed. She had a
rigid, cautious face and gray hair, brushed

smoothly down on either side of her forehead. She spoke with emphasis.

"You are right, Deacon Swain, Eunice has always had a *calling*, as I may say. From the time she was right small she was seriously inclined. She's a conscientious girl, if I *do* say it. It *was* a chance to go to the Continent to New York, and it weren't nothing to be governess to Mrs. Lane's children compared to teaching school here; but she had a call to stay here. She said she couldn't go off suddenly and leave everything at loose ends. She'd undertook the grammar-school, and this was her place."

Deacon Swain's face glowed with approval.

"Yet it *was* a chance to go to New York," he said, as if to provoke Mrs. Adams to further speech.

"So folks said," Mrs. Adams answered, dryly. "But Eunice only said as she didn't know as they *needed* her over to the Continent, and they did here, so 'twas her duty to stay."

By "Continent" a Nantucketer always means the mainland. Mrs. Adams paused, and then resumed, with a slight change of tone,

"Have you called a minister yet?"

" Well—no—" replied the deacon.

"Should think you'd best be hurryin' up," said Mrs. Adams, with some severity. "It's a cryin' disgrace that the Congregational Church of Nantucket should be so long without a minister. There's a fallin' away, and it'll grow. I heard of Maria Barnes and all the Aaron Macys at the Episcopal Church last Sunday."

The deacon looked uneasy.

"That's so," he assented; but he added, guardedly, "We had a meetin' yesterday, and we're bringin' matters to a p'int 's quick 's we can. Where's Eunice ?" he concluded.

"Out in the back lot, parin' apples for apple-butter," Mrs. Adams answered.

There was a pause of a few moments, while the two rockers creaked in concert.

"How does your boarder suit ?" inquired the deacon at last.

The cautious expression deepened in Mrs. Adams's face.

"Well enough !" she said, shortly.

The deacon looked at her with mild yet active curiosity.

" Does he—um—pay regular ?"

"Yes, he *pays* regular enough," Mrs. Adams admitted.

The deacon gazed meditatively at the ceiling. He did not wish to appear eager, yet he was anxious to discover the secret of Mrs. Adams's dissatisfaction with her lodger.

"I must say the young man commends himself strongly to me," he said. "He came into my store for some cigars the day he come, and he didn't seem much to like Nantucket. He'd took a room to the Springfield House. He's kind of foreign and openspoken, you know. He said he didn't want to stay to a hotel, when he came to Nantucket, with a lot of *tourists*. That's what he called the strangers."

The deacon laughed gently as he made this comment.

"Said he'd come to study the place and inhabitants; that what he wanted was *local coloring*. I've been a-kinder ponderin' that term ever since. Thought he'd go back to the Continent right off. 'Now,' says I"—the deacon was warming to his subject, for Mrs. Adams had stopped working and regarded him with deep attention—"says I, 'don't cross the bay to-day, it's as rugged as fury; stay a few days and you'll shake down. You see,' I says, 'this is a corner grocery, and folks drop in afternoons and it's real social. You're welcome,' I says, 'to

come in and get weighed as many times a
day's you want.' He seemed kinder pleased,
and then he wanted me to recommend him
to some private house, in a quiet street,
where he could take a room; and I told him
about you, for Eunice said you was thinking
about taking a boarder. I'm sorry he don't
suit."

He paused diplomatically. Mrs. Adams
began to sew again.

"Tain't that he doesn't suit," she said.
"He's *taking* enough; but it's against con-
science, my keepin' him. He's a godless,
Sabbath-breakin' man!"

She uttered this terrible accusation in a
calm, dry voice.

"You don't say!" said the deacon, breath-
lessly. His face was unaffectedly regretful.
"Yet," he continued, "he's full of natural
grace."

"Natural grace ain't goin' to help a man
where his eternal salvation is concerned,"
Mrs. Adams returned, severely. "You know
that, deacon, as well as I do."

The deacon made an unwilling movement
of assent with his head. "Yes, we are
taught so," he said, musingly; "and yet it
seems strange, for we are all made in the
image of God."

Mrs. Adams was too much occupied with her own thoughts to heed him.

"The question is," she continued, "whether, as the wife of a Presbyterian minister, I am justified in keeping him in my house."

The old man looked distressed. "It's a question, it's a question," he said; "but what makes you think he's—in an unregenerate state?"

"Plenty of things. He ain't much in the habit of making friends with strangers; but after he came I told him that, though we wouldn't vacate the sittin'-room for any one, he was welcome to come in and sit and play on the music. I *do* say he makes a sight of music come out of that melodeon; sounds like the organ I heard when I was to Boston with Ephraim."

"Yes," nodded the old man, "I remember your mentioning it to Lucilla when you came back to the Island."

"Well," said Mrs. Adams, "Sundays Dr. Otto played and sang same's other days, and such music! I can't liken it to anything I ever heard. It sounded, well—"

"French?" suggested the deacon. His imagination had been fired by the widow's eloquence, and the word came patly to his lips.

Mrs. Adams gave his eager, simple old face a sharp look over her glasses.

"Persian, more likely," she said, shortly. "Heathenish, anyhow. I soon put an end to that; but that ain't all. He works at his paintin's all day Sundays. He let fall in conversation that he makes a habit of attendin' the play. In Germany he had a seat regular, same as we have a pew in church. As far 's I can see he has no Bible. The other day I gave him Ephraim's tract, 'Going to the Play,' you know." The elder nodded. "He was polite enough to me about it; but when I came in after, he was readin' it, and as far as I could make out he was laughing. It just showed his feelings on sacred subjects."

A look of helpless distress had come into the deacon's face.

"What does Eunice say?" he asked.

"Well, Eunice always looks at things in a high kind of way. When I spoke to her she only says, 'Mother, perhaps his comin' here is a leadin' of Providence, and we ought not to bar the way.' That was three weeks ago. I don't know *how* she feels now."

The old man seemed relieved. "Eunice ain't likely to be far wrong in such matters.

The things of God are spiritually discerned, and it is given to such as her to discern them." He rose and took his hat from the table. "I must be goin' along." He shook hands somewhat limply with Mrs. Adams, who did not rise from the chair. "You'd better let Eunice settle that matter." His face became very grave and tender. "Eunice is one of the Elect, as I said before. It's my belief, Mrs. Adams, that the Lord has great things in store for her."

Mrs. Adams only gave him another scrutinizing glance. He left the room, and, as he let himself out of the door, she resumed her work, only calling to him,

"I'll send Lucilla some of my apple-butter; she told me she wa'n't preservin' this season."

The back porch of the house looked out on a small enclosure of sandy grass. There was but one stunted tree and no flowers. The gabled end of a neighboring house, painted a dull red, jutted out beyond the rickety fence, at one end of the enclosure. Beyond could be seen the windmill, on its mound, and the green moors. The atmosphere was so clear and sparkling that it lent an actual beauty to the very simple elements which made up this scene.

In the porch a man sat before his easel, painting. He had evidently intended to paint simply the gable of the house, with the glimpse of the windmill and the moor beyond—but Eunice Adams stood at a table just beyond the porch. On the table lay a pile of rusty-yellow and red apples, which she was paring. The background of the red house threw her figure into relief, and the temptation to add it to his picture was too strong for Dr. Julius Otto. He had sketched in her figure hastily, and was working carefully on the face. He seemed to be about thirty-five. His light-brown hair grew straight up from his forehead in a thick mass. His moustache swept away from his mouth in a bold wave. His beard was parted in the Prussian fashion, and he had a slightly obstinate mouth and chin. In the turn of his head, the expression of his eyes, in his whole manner, there was an enormous naturalness that was almost startling. He was speaking in rapid, fluent English, with a marked German accent.

"For my part," he said, " I am glad I am going to Vienna. I have been five years in this country, and it has treated me kindly. But I find you Americans too prejudiced, too narrow. Now, if you, for instance, could shake off some of the Puritanism that is blighting your life, you would be far happier."

He threw off this suggestion in a half-teasing manner, yet with a vivid heartiness that was like a cordial.

Eunice remained silent for a moment. Then she spoke with an effort.

" It is not always necessary to be happy."

Her face was one of those we sometimes see in New England. Her forehead was somewhat high, and her features had the same regularity that in her mother had hardened into rigidity. Her skin was colorless, and her dark hair was twisted in a heavy, waveless mass at the back of her head. Her eyes were singularly clear gray, with dark lashes and eyebrows. Her face had much beauty; but, more than this, it was so refined and spiritualized by some inward experience and habitual moral loftiness that it made a vivid impression on those who saw it for the first time. The Nantucketers were accustomed to this quality in her face, and took it as a matter of course; but the summer visitors who met her in the street used to wonder at the strange, exquisite face, afterwards remembering its transparent lambency of expression as something rarer and more exquisite than beauty.

Dr. Otto received her remark with a sort of kindly amusement.

"Why, if you please, Miss Eunice, is it not necessary to be happy?"

Eunice looked at him anxiously as he bent over his easel. She seemed to force herself to speak.

"Because, if we do our duty, it makes no difference whether we are happy or not. Things may seem hard here, but in another life—" She stopped suddenly, catching her breath nervously.

Dr. Otto's face had an expression of half-pitying protest.

"All very well," he said, with the same heartiness, "if one could be guaranteed the second lease. But you know we are only sure of *one* life!"

He laughed good-humoredly as he spoke.

The girl's face only became slightly paler. She dropped the knife and apple she held in her hands.

"Do not say that!" she said, in a low voice. "Every one can be sure. You *do* believe that?"

Her voice was so urgent that the German spoke with more seriousness.

"Really, Miss Eunice, do you wish me to speak the truth ?"

"Yes," she answered.

"Well, then, I will tell you frankly, I have long since arranged my life without reference to any such beliefs."

"How can you live, then?" Her eyes dilated as she looked at him.

"All the better," he answered, "since I have ceased to support or torment myself with false hopes or fears. The world is wide. There is so much to do, so much to live for, that there is more than scope for the largest intelligence. It satisfies me. If I complain and wish for more, I am not worthy to have standing-room. Out of it, and let some better man take my place! But I have not come to that yet. It is true there is misery and suffering, but we can all help each other. Let us do our duty. Yes—but let us be happy also, and not starve our lives as you do."

Eunice had remained motionless—then she spoke again in the same low voice.

"Do you mean to say you have no hope of immortality?"

Otto laughed.

"My dear Miss Eunice," he said, gently, "spend six months in a dissecting-room, and your ideas of life and immortality will undergo a startling change."

His words seemed to give Eunice a momentary insight into his habits of thought. Her face was strangely illuminated as she answered,

"It does no good to talk about it, Dr. Otto. It is not in my power that you shall or shall not believe. But the spirit of God is stronger than the mind or will of man. It can teach you and lead you as I cannot, as your own understanding cannot—whether you believe it or not, this is true."

At any other moment of his life Otto would have looked upon such an outburst as a pitiable exhibition of superstition. But perfect sincerity has a power of its own, and he was strangely impressed. To his surprise, Eunice suddenly gathered up the basket of apples and went rapidly into the house. As she passed him he saw that tears were streaming down her face. Their talk was only one of many, but none had reached this point. He whistled very softly to himself, and then went on painting in silence. Dr. Otto had little instinctive reverence, or, as he would have expressed it, no superstitions; but he had broad sympa-

thies and a tender heart. He began to regret having spoken so frankly.

At meals Eunice first served her mother
and their guest, and then took her own seat
at the table. When he first came this proceeding was highly embarrassing to Otto.
If Eunice had been less educated and less refined, it would not have seemed so incongru-
ous. He used to jump up from his seat to
assist her; but he found that this was only
disturbing to both Mrs. Adams and her
daughter, and he now submitted with a
good grace. This evening Eunice was un-
usually quiet. Long before now Otto had
learned the secret of waking her laughter.
It had a fresh, unused sweetness, and he
learned to wait for this sound and to enjoy
it genuinely when it came. But now this
pleasure was not in store for him. The
girl's eyes were swollen from crying, and
her manner was full of the dignity of a
quiet sorrow. After supper Mrs. Adams
took her seat in the rocking-chair of the
living-room, with her knitting. Eunice was
clearing away the dishes. Otto, who had
lingered in the room, spoke suddenly to her.

"Miss Eunice, I am afraid my thought-
less remarks this afternoon have troubled
you?"

9

She made no reply, but stood with her eyes cast down. He went on with his usual fluency,

"Even if one has no household gods, one should not try to knock down one's neighbor's. I have no desire to shake your faith. I have no creed to offer you in exchange but the very finite one I proposed this afternoon"—he broke off—"in fact, I can only ask you to forgive me."

She looked up quietly, and he saw that, in spite of her reddened eyes, her expression was lofty and collected.

"You have not shaken my faith. It is only terrible to know that you—that any one should feel as you do. If you were ignorant, it would be different"—she stopped—"but it does no good to talk about it." She took a dish from the table and left the room.

Otto, a little baffled, went into his own room and lighted his lamp. Mrs. Adams and Eunice had arranged this room with their own hands. The walls were white-washed, and a square of blue and gray ingrain carpeting covered the floor. The drop-shades were of thick light-blue paper, and the window-curtains of blue and white mosquito-netting, looped back with a wide

strip of the blue paper of 'which the shades
were made. The furniture was of the cheap-
est painted wood, with the exception of a
mahogany bureau with small brass knobs.

Above the looking-glass hung a worsted-
work sampler, framed, and covered with
glass. There was an inscription thereon
to this effect :

"Mary Folger is my name,
America is my nation;
Nantucket is my dwelling-place,
And Christ is my salvation."

The figure of the German was in curious
contrast to the air of humble sanctity which
this room possessed. He looked too large
for its small proportions, and too aggressive
for its timid propriety. His tweed shoot-
ing-jacket and a pair of muddy corduroys
sprawled over a chair, where he had flung
them when he came in from a sketching expedition the day before. His portfolio lay
open on the table, and he sat down by it
and looked at his sketches. They seemed
to him monotonous—some of the most char-
acteristic Nantucket houses; one or two of
the narrowest and crookedest lanes; and
the rest of the moors, always the moors. At
sunset, in the golden haze of the setting sun;
at twilight, purpled and shadowy; at dawn,

by Tom Never's Head, the brown moor and the still sea reddened with the flush of the morning.

For a moment they brought back the perfect reality woven into his mental fibres by the tenderest thoughts of his life; then they seemed only faded reflections. He pushed them aside almost angrily.

He had graduated from a medical college in Berlin as a physician some years before; but after a couple of years he gave up his practice, and became an artist from sheer inability to keep out of his studio when he should have been cultivating the good-will of his patients. He came to America, and although he made little money, his artistic reputation induced his friends in Germany to secure for him the position of professor of drawing in the principal art school of Vienna.

He was to sail in a month more, and had come to Nantucket to sketch, as well as for a rest before sailing. Now, as the weeks passed, Dr. Otto realized that he was painfully unwilling to go away. He was almost impatient of this feeling, yet he could not overcome it. The remote oddity of the place and people, with one exception, were repugnant to him. The fact that the little island was sea-girt and thirty miles from

the mainland gave him a sense of confine-
ment. The four walls of his room seemed
to suffocate him. He started up and opened
the door of his room. The chill September
air blew in at the open hall door.

"I shall sail two weeks earlier," thought
Otto, "and go to Italy for a fortnight before
going to Vienna."

He went into the sitting-room. It was
deserted. He heard Mrs. Adams moving
about in the kitchen. Eunice was nowhere
to be seen. He sat down at the open melodeon and played and sang the *Mignon's Lied*
of Liszt.

"Kennst du das Land wo die Citronen blüh'n
Im dunkeln Laub die Gold-Orangen glüh'n?"

floated out through the open door into a
room across the hall, where Eunice Adams
sat at a table piled with books and papers.
She was correcting the children's exercises
for the next day. She had not been at the
Nantucket high-school, nor had the run of
the town library, for nothing. She understood the words Otto sang. The mellow,
pleading tones seemed to curl around her
heart and sink into it.

"Kennst du es wohl?
Dahin! Dahin! möcht' ich mit dir, O mein Gelieb-
ter, ziehn."

After a moment she got up, walked firmly across the hall, and softly closed the door of the sitting-room; and, coming back, shut and bolted the door of her own room. In the slightly built house the music still sounded, but she bent her head in her hands as she sat by the table, and then went on slowly and patiently with her task.

Dr. Otto was beginning to enjoy thoroughly his own music. He made the little instrument tremble and vibrate and give forth grandly the rich harmonies of the song. He sang with feeling, with soul. Suddenly he heard the door shut gently, and footsteps retreat across the hall and the shutting of a second door. He sprang from his chair.

"Barbarians!" he muttered in German, "they do not even appreciate good music."

Then he laughed, and, shutting the melodeon, looked at his watch and yawned—nine o'clock.

Mrs. Adams put out the light in the dining-room and looked suspiciously into the sitting-room.

"Oh, you can put the light out here," said Otto, apologetically, as if he had been discovered in a crime.

"I s'pose I might as well," said Mrs. Adams, dryly. "It's gettin' late."

"Late! O ye gods!" murmured Otto.

He went down the passage to his room and went meekly to bed.

II.

Two or three days later Otto was standing at the window of the sitting-room. As he looked down the road he saw Eunice Adams coming towards the house with a young man. They were in earnest conversation. The stranger was evidently a clergyman, from his provincially clerical dress and white cravat. He was tall and slender, with a thin, intellectual face, a long nose, and meditative blue eyes. Otto saw a look of deep affection and respect in these eyes as the young man bent them on Eunice. Otto turned abruptly away from the window, and, taking his hat and sketching materials from the table, went out into the hall, meeting Eunice and her companion as they entered. Eunice looked at him with vague anxiety. To his surprise she spoke to him.

"Are you going out, Dr. Otto? Dinner will be ready in a few minutes."

"I shall not be at home to dinner. I am going out to sketch," he replied.

He almost brushed by the young clergyman, who stood against the wall of the narrow hall to let him pass, and left the house. A half an hour later his cheeks tingled at the recollection of his childishness. "Blockhead!" he muttered to himself, "thou art not a boy, why shouldst thou care?" and later, "Why not have waited and found out—"

Otto managed to get some dinner at a farm-house on the moors that day. Something seemed to be dragging him back to the little house in Vestal Street, but he obstinately prolonged his own suspense. He made sketch after sketch, painstaking and laborious, and ended by destroying them all.

In a sort of inward vision he had seen all day the figures of Eunice and the young clergyman. It was dark when he reached the town, at last, worn out with his long struggle with himself. The moon had come out and bathed the still, white streets with its pure light. It was as still and warm as a midsummer night. The houses looked blanker than ever as he passed them. As he neared the Adams house he saw a figure

approaching him; small, and walking with
a tremulous step; his head was uncovered,
and his white locks floated in a silver aure-
ole as he came towards him. He held a tall
bunch of white, feathery grasses in his hand,
and looked not unlike an elderly Angel of
the Annunciation. It was Deacon Swain.
He moved his hat into his left hand, and
held out his right in greeting to the younger man. His face shone with a gentle radiance as he looked up at him.

"A beautiful night, doctor," he said.

Otto assented. The old man looked up
at the night sky.

"It reminds me of the hymn we sang last
Sunday," he said.

> "'Soon as the evening shades prevail
> The moon takes up the wondrous tale,
> And nightly to the listening earth
> Repeats the story of her birth;
> And all the stars that round her burn,
> And all the planets in their turn,
> Confirm the tidings as they roll,
> And spread the truth from pole to pole.'

"It seems as though such nights as this
came to show us that God's mercy to mankind is as boundless as His universe." He
put on his hat as he ended. "Good-night,
doctor," he said, and passed on.

Otto's footsteps made no sound on the
sandy path as he reached the house. At
the gate beyond the house, which led into
the "pasture," as the enclosure was called,
stood two figures. In the moonlight Otto
recognized them as the realization of his
vision that day. The man held Eunice's
hand in his, and she looked at him earnest-
ly. Otto stood still for an instant; then he
turned quickly aside, and going up the three
steps which led to the door, opened it and
went in. Mrs. Adams confronted him in
the hall with a startled face.

"How you scart me!" she exclaimed.
"You came in so quiet. There's a letter for
you here," she continued.

She led the way into the sitting-room,
and Otto followed.

The letter was a brief summons from the
directors of the art school, requesting him
to come to Vienna to begin his duties at
once. As he stood by the table reading the
letter, Mrs. Adams went on speaking. Every word she said pierced his consciousness
like an electric shock.

"It was a pity you wa'n't in to-day. My
nephew, the Rev. Amos Lathrop, was here.
He came over from Wood's Holl for the day,
and his conversation is of a nature to im-

prove the most hardened person. Deacon
Swain came in to tea, and he and Amos and
Eunice talked. It reminded me of the mil-
lennium. Amos planned to bring his wife
with him, but she couldn't leave the children."

Mrs. Adams turned to go out.
" Have you had your supper?" she added.
" Because, if you haven't, Eunice saved some
for you."

She left the room without waiting for a
reply.

Otto stood motionless by the table for a
moment. Then he threw back his head and
laughed — a low, happy laugh. He went
out in the hall to the open door at the back
of the house. A figure stood in the moonlight near the porch. It was Eunice. He
went towards her. His happiness at the
sight of her overflowed in his eyes and whole
expression. In the moonlight her features
had an ineffable suavity and purity. She
spoke to him gently.

"You have come back. I'm sorry you
could not have talked to my cousin, who
has been here all day."

Otto almost laughed at the earnest anxiety of her look and words. What were the
speculations of a worn-out theology to him

compared with the reality of his love? It
carried him on like a great tide. Its strength
must carry Eunice with it.

A half-hour later Mrs. Adams was sitting in her room, reading her Bible, when
Eunice came and stood before her. Mrs.
Adams closed her Bible, keeping one of her
fingers between the pages as a mark, and
looked up at her daughter. Eunice was
very pale, and her manner was filled with
an intense, controlled excitement.

"Well?" said Mrs. Adams, calmly.

"Mother, Dr. Otto is going away."

"Well?" said Mrs. Adams again.

Eunice turned her head away, and her
voice sank. Her mother watched her with
immovable confidence.

"He asked me to marry him and go with
him." She waited a moment, and went on
slowly: "I told him I could never marry an
unbeliever; and more, that my life was promised for another service."

Mrs. Adams opened her Bible at the place
where her finger divided the pages. She
read aloud with emphasis:

"'No man having put his hand to the
plough and looking back is fit for the king-
dom of God.'" She turned the pages and

read again : "'Be ye not unequally yoked together with unbelievers.'"

"I know," said Eunice. The words came with a deep expiration of her breath, a sigh that was like a renunciation of her whole nature. She turned away, and slowly left the room.

The next morning Otto waked late. In spite of the confident spirit of mastery in which he had finally fallen asleep, he awoke with a feeling of overpowering desolation, and found his eyes wet with tears, a thing which was so novel that it startled him. The rebuff of the night before was puzzling, and he began to feel that there might be something in Eunice's theology which was stronger than he, stronger than herself. By the time he was dressed he had reasoned away his fears. It was Saturday, and he congratulated himself, with a sense of triumph, that there was no school that day or the next, and that Eunice would be free. He found his breakfast saved for him in the dining-room; the striped cotton cloth turned back at one end and his plate laid on the unpainted wood. Eunice was nowhere to be seen. Mrs. Adams came into the room. He was not in a mood for *finesse*.

"Mrs. Adams, where is Miss Eunice?" he asked, abruptly.

Mrs. Adams looked at him inscrutably.

"Eunice is over to Surfside, to my sister Mrs. Burdick's. She's gone for Sunday."

On Monday Otto was going. His pride was stung, and he made his preparations to go away. If the desire of his heart was to be unfulfilled, he would burn his ships behind him. He would go without seeing Eunice again. Twice on Sunday he watched Mrs. Adams, in her rusty black dress and bonnet, go down the sandy road on her way to church. The warm weather still held, and the sun shone through a golden September haze. In spite of this sunshine in the still, darkened house and glaring, shadowless street, life and hope seemed dead. Otto thought of Eunice, with her violin-soul waiting for the strings to be touched, and then of Vestal Street, and the grammar-school—forever! Why should such things be? Then passion and hope rushed back in a warm, indignant tide. He would not give her up. . . .

The last rays of sunlight bathed the sea. The bronze moors were laid with cloth of gold. At the western horizon the sun's own majesty was lost in a blaze of transparent light.

Eunice Adams stood in the porch of her aunt's house with Deacon Swain. His box-cart stood before the house. Eunice's face was turned towards the sun, but she did not see it. The light touched the white hair of the old man as he stood before her.

He held her hand in his.

"You have decided, then. The Lord has called you, Eunice," he said, with tremulous solemnity. "Thank God that your ears have not been closed, but, like Samuel, you have heard and answered His voice. I always said He had great things in store for you."

He turned away, and, getting into his cart, drove away.

Eunice looked out on the sea, rapt in a peace from which there seemed no recall. The future seemed to her like the path of light from the setting sun on the Western sea—lonely, perhaps, but clearly defined, and ending in a glorious infinity. A sound aroused her. She looked and saw Otto standing before her. To see him there was like the sound of a loved voice calling from earth to a ransomed soul in bliss.

He told her he was going away; that he

must speak to her before leaving. He spoke
in abrupt, short sentences, almost in gasps.
With her calm, glorified face she seemed to
be slipping away from him.

"What is the use?" said Eunice, slowly.
"Do not ask me to listen."

In her quiet resistance he felt the hopeless-
ness of the early morning stealing over him.

He began to speak with enforced self-
control.

"You are sacrificing yourself—me—to
some principle—some idea—which has no
reasonable foundation." His German accent
became stronger than ever as he rolled out
these words. "Why should you not be
happy? You are young—"

"I am twenty-eight," Eunice interrupted
with mechanical truth. Her lips had become
very white.

"It is cruel," Otto began, vehemently.
He stopped abruptly.

With one hand he had grasped the post of
the porch; the other hung at his side. He
turned away and looked out over the sea.
The glory had faded, and there was only a
gray expanse of water.

"I have made a mistake," he said, heavi-
ly; "I thought perhaps you loved me a little."

Eunice stood with her hands clasped
tightly, her eyes fixed on his face. She suddenly caught the hand that hung by his side
and pressed it against her heart, and then
raised it to her lips. In her face was an
agony of love and renunciation.

"You don't understand," she murmured;
"I must do what is right." She seemed
about to say more, but before she could do
so a third person came from the house into
the porch—a middle-aged woman, sallow
and dark-eyed. She looked sharply at Eunice and Otto.

"Won't you ask yer company into the
house, Eunice?" she said, reproachfully.

"Yes, Aunt Eunice," she said, faintly.
"This is mother's boarder—Dr. Otto—please
excuse me, I do not feel well."

She left them, and, going into the house,
went wearily up the narrow stairs to her
room.

"Come in and take a seat, doctor," said
Mrs. Burdick.

Otto waited ten minutes while Mrs. Burdick subjected him to a cross-questioning;
at the end of it she decided there was
"something between" Eunice and "doctor."
Then at Otto's request she went to call her
niece. After a few minutes she came back
10

with a message that her niece was not well, and was sorry she could not see him again.

"I s'pose you'd like to know about Eunice's plans, doctor," she said; "I could tell you," said Mrs. Burdick, peering sharply at him in the dim light.

But Dr. Otto seemed in no mood for listening, and after a brief good-night he walked away over the darkening moors. From a window in the farm-house some one watched him through blinding tears. The next morning he had left Nantucket.

It was curious that, after a month of rusticating, Dr. Otto should have been seized with a low, nervous fever. Instead of sailing for Germany he remained with an artist friend, who took care of him until he was well enough to go out again. It was Friday, three weeks after he had left Nantucket; his passage in a German steamer was taken for the following Wednesday. It has been said that he was well enough to go out, and Saturday evening found him again in Nantucket. He had overrated his strength, and when he arrived at the hotel his head swam and throbbed with a dizzy weakness. It conquered his impulses, and he was obliged to

go to bed and toss about all night and all
the next day, half blind with headache and
fever. Towards evening the pain ebbed away.
He dressed, ordered a cup of hot coffee,
drank it, and felt that his nerves were steady
once more. He waited until he knew that
the Adams's supper-hour was past, and then
took a carriage and drove to Vestal Street.
The church-bells were ringing for evening
service as he drove through the dark streets.
The sparkling October air refreshed him.
When he reached the silent house he got
out and rang the bell, his heart beating
wildly. There was no answer; he rang again,
and waited with a vague apprehension. The
driver suggested that "perhaps the folks was
to evening church." Otto smiled at his for-
getfulness. He would drive to the church
and wait in the last pew until Eunice came
out, and then—

When he reached the church Otto dismissed the carriage and slipped silently into the
last pew. The lights at the back were dim.
The sermon was just ending. There was perfect stillness except a single voice. This
voice gave Otto a strange thrill. He thought
he was dreaming. Eunice Adams stood in
the pulpit speaking in a low tone of entreaty,
a slight figure in a black dress. Her face was

pale, but it was illumined as from an inward radiance.

Otto only received a bewildered impression of the self-forgetful tenderness of her face as she pleaded with the listening people before her, dedicating her life to the mission of their salvation. She ceased speaking, and, clasping her hands, looked upward. There was a breathless hush; then the congregation bowed their heads for the closing prayer. In the rustle of the bending forms Otto left the church. His brain was in a turmoil. He seemed to hear in the air around him a voice saying, *"Your God is not my God, nor your ways my ways."* . . .

He made no effort to see her again.

The next morning Otto sat on the deck of the boat as it steamed out of the Nantucket harbor. He felt strangely weak and quiet. He watched the gray town, throned like a queen on the rising ground of the island. The shore became blurred as the boat travelled silently over the shining water. The town sank as the distance from it became greater, until at length there was only a faint white line on the horizon where the blue sea met the blue sky. A few smoke-wreaths shadowed the sky above the place where the town had been. At length they, too, had vanished. Only the sea glittered under the sun.

A sick man has strange fancies. Had the island ever been there? Perhaps, like Eunice's God, the island — Eunice herself — were dreams. Yes, but Eunice and the island existed although he could not see them. Why should not the same be true of . . .? Eunice seemed cruel, but perhaps they would both understand some day. Pshaw! the light dazzled his eyes. He would go to sleep. Dr. Otto pulled his hat over his eyes and slept; or, at least, the pilot, who sat just above him in his little house, thought he did.

A SPEAKIN' GHOST.

BY MRS. ANNIE TRUMBULL SLOSSON.

YES, I do b'lieve in 'em—in one of 'em, tennerate. An' I know why you ask me if I do. Somebody's put you up to it, so 's you can make me tell my ghost story. Well, you're welcome to that if you want it. It's no great of a story, but it's true; an', arter all, that's the main p'int in a story—ghost or no ghost.

Well, I s'pose I'll s'prise you when I say it all happened in New York city. Seein' me here in Kitt'ry, an' knowin' my name's Jenness—a real Kitt'ry an' Portsmouth an' Rye name—why, o'course you'd take it for granted I'd allers lived round here, an' all my happenin's had been in this local'ty. Well, you're right one way. I was born about here, an' come of good old Scataqua River stock. My father was Andronicus Jenness, born an' raised in Rye, and the fust thing I rec'lect we was livin' in

Portsmouth, on the old Odiorne's P'int
road.

There was father 'n' mother, three boys
—Amos, Ezry, an' Peleg—an' me, Mary Ann,
the oldest o' the family an' the only girl.
It's the ghost story you want to hear, so I
ain't goin' to bother you with anything else.

But that time I lived there in the old red
house, with my own folks round me—'pears
to me now the only time I did ever reely
live. We was pretty well to do, we had a
good home, and we was all together. Father was a good man, mother the very best
o' women, an' I was dreffle fond on 'em.
An' the boys, they was just rugged, noisy,
good - natur'd chaps, that kep' the house
lively enough, I can tell you. But when I
was nigh on to twenty-five, an' the boys was
twenty an' seventeen an' fifteen, it all ended,
that life in the old red house. Father an'
my three laughin', high-sperrited, pleasant-
spoken boys, was all drownded at once, one
day in September. They went out in a sail-
boat, a storm come up—'twas the beginnin'
of the line gale—an' their boat capsized;
an' them that went out rugged an' big an'
healthy, laughin' back at ma an' me as we
stood at the door to see 'em off, was fetched
back stiff an' wet an' cold, an' so dreffle still.

I never'd seen the boys still afore in all their lives.

Mother never held up her head arter that day, an' afore the new year come in she'd follered pa an' the boys. It left me dreffle lonesome. You couldn't 'a' broke up a fam'ly in all that section that 'd 'a' took it harder. For we'd allers set so much by each other, an' done ary thing we could to keep together an' not be sep'rated, an' there we was, all broke up at once, an' the old house nothin' now but a dry holler shell. I didn't want, o' course, to rattle round in it longer'n I could help. I got red on it's fast as I could, an' went over to Rye. I knowed how to work an' wa'n't afraid of it, an', o' course, the more I had to do just then the better for me. For I was stupid an' scared an' sore with the dreffle trouble that come on me so quick an' suddin, an' I was so terr'ble lonesome.

Well, I s'pose 'twas because I'd allers liked boys, an' was used to havin' 'em round, an' because, too, o' my missin' my own boys so bad, that I got a place at fust in Mr. Sheaf's school. 'Twas a boys' school, an' they took me for a kind of house-keeper— to see to things generally. 'Twas a sort of comfort—as much as anything in this world

could be a comfort—to see the boys an' do
for 'em. I had a little place to myself right
off the school-room, an' there I used to do
my mendin' an' everything I could contrive
to do for an excuse to stay right there, where
I could see an' hear them boys. 'Twas a
kind of eddication jest to hear 'em go over
their lessons—their jography an' rethmetic
an' grammar—an' partikly their readin' an'
sayin' pieces. Ev'ry speakin' day—Friday
'twas—I was allers on hand, never losin' a
word, an' sometimes I'd practise the boys
'forehand till they knowed their pieces perfect. I stayed there about six months, an' I
hoped I could stay there the rest o' my days.
But even that poor comfort had to be took
away; for Mr. Sheaf's health broke down;
he give up the school an' moved away. So
I lost even them borrered boys, who'd been
in a sort o' way helpin' to fill up the places
o' my own. An' so agin I was left terr'ble
lonesome. I didn't know what to do, nor
care much. So, when I had an opp'tunity
to go to New York I took it.

'Twas a lady who'd had a boy at the school,
an' had been there herself an' seen me. Mis'
Davis she was, an' she writ to know if I'd
come on to stay in her house through the
summer, an' do for her pa while she an' her

children was off to the country. As I said
afore, I didn't much care what I done, I was
so lonesome an' mis'rable; so I said I'd go.

But if I'd been lonesome afore, I was a
hunderd times lonesomer there. I never 'd
been in a big city afore, an' I'd kind o'
thought 'twould be folksy an' 'livenin' an'
cheerful. But 'twa'n't a mite like that.
The house was mostly shet up an' dark.
Mr. Rice—Mis' Davis's pa—was off all day
long, took his dinner an' supper to a tavern
somewheres, an' was only to home to sleep
an' eat his breakfast. I didn't have much
of anything to do. I had a big down-stairs
room they called the front basement to set
in. It had two windows on the street, but
'twas so low down that you couldn't see
much out of 'em without screwin' your neck
an' peekin' up. There was lots o' folks
passin' by all the time, but you couldn't
scasly see anything but their feet an' legs.
An' oh, the noise o' the wagons an' cars! It
made me 'most crazy at first, but bimeby I
got a little used to it. But I thought I
should jest die o' homesickness. How I'd
think an' think an' think o' the old days an'
the old house on the Odiorne's P'int road!
How diff'rent it was from this city one!
The old home was so quiet an' still outside,

an' so noisy an' lively in-doors; an' the city
house was so noisy an' lively out-doors, an'
so dreffle still an' quiet inside.

An' 'twas right there in the front basement o' that city house that I see the ghost.
'Twa'n't like ary other ghost I ever heerd on.
Them I've read about mostly wore white
sheets, an' looked dreffle skully an' bony, an'
kind o' awful. One o' that sort would 'a'
scaret me, I know; but this one — why, I
never felt a mite scaret from the very fust.
Fact is, I never knowed 'twas a ghost for a
spell, for it looked like a boy, jest a common,
ord'nary boy; an' 'twas a speakin' one. I
don't mean one that talked, but a speakin'
one that spoke pieces.

I don't think I smelt pepp'mint the fust
time it come. I don't rec'lect it anyway,
but allers arter that I did. I was settin' in
the front basement when it come. 'Twas
between five an' six in the arternoon, light
enough still out-doors, but kind o' dusky
in my down-stairs room. I wasn't doin'
anything jest then but settin' in my chair
an' thinkin'. I don't know what 'twas exackly that made me look up an' across the
room, but I done it; an' there, standin' right
near the table an' lookin' at me, was the
ghost; though, 's I said afore, I didn't know

it for a ghost then; it looked like a boy.
But he wasn't a city boy, nor like any one
I'd seen for a long spell. He was about
fourteen or fifteen, I should think, an' he
wa'n't no way pretty to look at, but I liked
him from the fust minute. He was real
freckled, but that never was a great draw-
back to me; an' he had kind o' light, reddish-yeller hair, not very slick, but mussy
an' rough like. His eyes was whity-blue,
an' he hadn't much in the way o' eye-wink-
ers or eyebrows. An' his nose was kind o'
wide, an' jest a mask o' freckles, like a turkey egg. So, you see, he wa'n't much to
look at for beauty, but I took to him right
off. I knowed he was from the country 's
soon as I see him. Any one could tell that.
His hands was red an' rough an' scratched,
an' he had warts. Then his clothes showed
it too. You could see in a jiffy they was
home-made, an' cut over and down from his
pa's. There was a sort o' New Hampshire
look about him too, an' I felt a real drawin'
to him right off. I was jest a mite s'prised
to see him standin' there, for I hadn't heerd
a knock or anything, but afore I could speak
an' ask him what he wanted, he stepped up
in front o' me, an' says, sort o' quick an' excited like,

"Don't you want to hear me speak my piece?"

An' afore I had time to say that yes, bless his little heart, I jest would, he begun:

"My name is Norvle; on the crampin' hills
My father feeds his flock,"

an' a lot more about his folks, an' all so pretty spoken an' nice. When he'd done he drawed one foot up to t'other an' made a bow, real polite, an' then he stood stock-still agin. O' course I praised him up, said he'd spoke his piece beautiful, an' asked him if he wouldn't like a cooky. I got up an' went to the pantry to get some, but when I turned round to ask him if he liked sugar or m'lasses best, he'd gone. I thought 'twas pretty suddin, but then I s'posed he was bashful, an' had took that way o' leavin' to save talk an' fuss. I looked out o' the winder to see if he was round, but there wa'n't a sign on him, an' I give him up. An' 'twas jest then I begun to smell pepp'mint. But I didn't put the two things—the boy an' the pepp'-mint—together then; not till some time arterwards.

Well, you don't know how it chirked me up, that little visit. To be sure, it had been real short an' unsat'sfact'ry. He hadn't never told me one word about hisself—where he come from, who he was, nor anything. But that didn't seem to make no diff'rence to me. I felt 's if I knowed him real well, an' his folks afore him ; an' somehow, too, I had a feelin' that he'd come agin, an' I'd find out all I wanted to about him an' his belongin's. But thinkin' about him an' his call an' all made the time pass real quick, an' 'twas bed-time afore I knowed it — the fust evenin' sence I come there that I hadn't jest longed for nine, an' looked at the clock twenty times an hour.

The next day slipped by in the same slip-pety way, for I was goin' over in my mind what he'd done an' said, an' s'posin' an' s'po-sin' who his folks was, an' all that.

About the same time o' day, towards six o'clock or so, I set down in the same place by the winder an' begun to watch for him. He hadn't said he'd come, but I had a strong feelin' inside that he was goin' to. An' he did. But 'twa'n't out o' the winder I see him. For I begun to smell a strong pepp'-minty kind o' smell agin', an' I turned to look up at the shelf where I kept my med'cines to see if the bottle was broke or the stopple out, an' —there stood the ghost. Though even then I never dreamed 'twas a ghost.

I thought 'twas jest a boy. He was standin' across the room, jest where I fust see him,
by the table, an' lookin' straight at me. An'
afore I could say a word he started right for
me, an' says, lookin' real bright an' int'rested, "Don't you want to hear me speak my
piece?" An' off he went as glib as could be.
I can't, for the life o' me, rec'lect what 'twas
he spoke that time. I get the pieces mixed
somehow them days, afore the time come
when they meant somethin', an' I begun to
take in their meanin's. Mebbe 'twas

"At midnight when the sun was low,"

or it might be

"On Linden in his gardin tent,"

for I know he spoke them some time. Tennerate he said off something. An' when he'd
done he drawed up his foot an' bowed real
nice. I clapped my hands an' praised him
up, an' then I begun to ask questions. I
wanted to know what his name was, where
he come from, who his folks was, how he
knowed about me, why he come, an' lots o'
things. He stayed quite a long spell, an' I
did jest enjoy that talk. Bimeby I went
into the closet to get something to show

him, an' when I come back, he was gone
agin. 'Twa'n't till some time arter he'd left
that I rec'lected that though it seemed 's if
I'd had a good talk with him, I'd done it all
my own self, an' he never 'd said one single
word. Nothin', I mean, but that one thing
he allers said, " Don't you want to hear me
speak my piece ?"

An' yet somehow I knowed lots more about
him than afore. In the fust place, I'd come
to feel cert'in sure his name was Norvle, an'
that he wa'n't only speakin' a piece about
that, but meant it for gospel truth. An'
arter that I never thought o' him by any
other name. An' I did think o' him lots.
For even in them two little visits, when I'd
done most o' the talk myself, I'd got drefile
fond on him. You know I allers liked boys,
partikerly boys raised in the country dees-
tricks. An' up to this time an' quite a spell
arterwards I never guessed he was anything
but a boy, jest a common, ord'nary boy.
Well, he kept comin'.- Every single arternoon, jest about six o'clock, or a speck earlier or later, I begun to smell a sort o' pepp'-
minty smell, an' in come that boy, walked
up to me, with his eyes all shinin', lookin
pleased au' sort o' excited, an' says, " Don't
you want to hear me speak my piece ?"

Then he'd speak. They was diff'rent kinds
o' pieces; some was verses an' some wasn't.
But they was all nice, pretty pieces. There
was one I remember about a boy standin' on
the deck of a ship afire, an' how he stood
an' stood an' stood, an' wouldn't set down
a minute. Another r'lated to the breakin'
waves, an' how they dashed up real high.
An' there was a long one that didn't rhyme,
about Romans an' countrymen an' lovers;
he did speak that jest beautiful.

Then he'd hold out one arm straight an'
tell how nobody never heerd a drum nor a
fun'ral note the time they buried somebody
in a awful hurry. Agin he'd start off speech-
iflyin' about its bein' a real question arter all
whether you had'nt better be, or hadn't better not be. That one seemed to be a kind o'
riddle; not much sense to it. An' there was
a loud one where he jest insisted that our
chains is forged. "Their clankin'," he says,
"may be heerd on the plains o' Boston." I
b'lieve 'twas in that one he kep' a-sayin',
"Let it come; I repeat it, sir, let it come.
Gentlemen may cry peace, peace, but there
ain't no peace,' an' so on. Real el'quent
'twas, I hold.

An' I growed so proud o' that boy. By
this time I knowed a good deal about him,
11

for I'd have long talks with him 'most every day. That is, I thought I was havin' long talks with him; but allers, arter he'd gone, I'd rec'lect he hadn't really said anything. But temperate, strange as it seems, I did know lots more about him every time. As I said afore, his name was Norvle. His folks was plain farmin' people. You know he spoke of his pa's keepin' sheep the fust time he come. An' 'twas up in the mountains they lived; prob'ly somewheres in the White Mountains, this State. I know once he spoke o' Conway 's if he lived round there. That was in a piece about there bein' jest seven children in their fam'ly. He was real par-tikler about the quantity, an' kep' callin' at-tention to the fact that there was exackly seven; no more, no less. He says,

"Two of us at Conway dwells,
   An' two has gone to sea";

an' he went on to say,

"Two of us in the church-yard lays,"

(that was him an' another, I s'pose now, but still says he,

"Seven boys an' girls is we."

I was sorry he hadn't been brought up
near the water as my boys had, with the
great big sea to look at an' sail on. No
wonder he spoke o' the crampin' hills. It
allers seemed to me dreffle crampin' to be
shut up among the hills an' away from the
salt-water.

An' now he was off from home an' real
lonesome, so 'twas a comfort to him to
come over an' see me, a plain, self-respectin'
countrywoman, like his ma an' his aunts.
So I about made up my mind to take charge
on him, do for him, an'—if his folks would
let me—sort o' adopt him, in the place o' my
own boys layin' in Portsmouth graveyard.

I never 's long 's I live shall forgit the
day I found out he wa'n't a boy, a common,
ord'nary boy, but a ghost. He'd jest come
in, an' was sayin' his piece, when the grocer
come to the door with some things.

"Wait a minute, Norvle," I says, for I
did'nt like to lose a word of his speeches,
I liked 'em all so, an' I went to the door.
But as I opened it an' let the man in, I
heerd the boy goin' right on speakin'. So I
says to the grocer man, in a kind o' whisper,
beck'nin' as I spoke, "Jest come in an' hear
this boy!" For I was real proud of him, an'
glad o' a chance to show him off.

The man looked rather s'prised, but he follered me in, an' we both stood there by the door, list'nin' to the little feller. That is, *I* was list'nin' with all my ears, for 'twas one o' his very best, about England may 's well 'tempt a dam up the waters o' the Nile with bulrushes. But when I looked round at the man, smilin' at him an' noddin' my head, 's if to say, "Ain't he smart?" I see he wa'n't 'pearin' to hear anything 'tall. He was lookin' at me, an' then round, an' seemin' so dumfounndered.

"What's the matter o' you?" he says. "What's up?"

Norvle was jest closin' then, an' I waited till he'd made his bow, an' then I says agin, "Wait a minute, Norvle, an' then we'll have our talk." Then I turned round to the grocer, an' I says, "Don't he speak fust-rate?"

"What you talkin' about?" says he. "Got a sunstroke?"

Somehow I knowed all at once that he wa'n't foolin', an' that he didn't see nor hear what I see an' hear so plain, so plain. An' I knowed more'n that, for that one little thing opened my eyes that I jest wouldn't open till then, an' I couldn't shet 'em agin. I felt queer an' dizzy, my head swum, an' I

put out my hands to keep from fallin'. The
man stiddied me, helped me into my chair,
fetched me some water, an' I was well
enough arter a little to speak. I told him
I felt better, an' he could go; so he went
away. I looked for Norvle, but he wasn't
there. There was, jest a little smell o'
pepp'mint in the air, but the boy'd gone. I
was glad he had, for I wanted to be all
alone for a spell.

Well, you can't understand anything
about what I went through then; nobody
can. To folks I'm jest a queer old woman
who tells a com'cal ghost story out of her
stupid old head. It wa'n't very com'cal to
me that day. For I'd got so fond o' that
boy. I allers liked 'em; an' I'd lost all I
ever had. An' now this one had come to
me when I was so lonesome an' low in my
mind, an' I'd gone an' took him right into
my heart. An' he wa'n't a boy at all, but a
ghost! That meant so much. Queer 's it
seems, the fust thought that struck me was
this: he wa'n't *he* or *him*, but jest *it*. Then
I remembered how I'd planned some new
clothes for him. But ghosts don't wear out
their clothes. An' I'd meant—if his folks
would let me—to adopt him; bring him up
like my own. How ever could I adopt a

ghost? Wa'n't it impossible? Come to
think o' it, could I have dealin's in any way
with a ghost? We'd allers been a respect'ble fam'ly; none more so in all New
Hampshire; a religious fam'ly too, orth'dox,
every single one. Never, 's fur 's I'd heerd,
was there a ghost of any kind mixed up
with ary branch o' the Jennesses for gen'ra-
tions. To be sure, there was a story of one
that appeared to the Fosses, connected by
marriage with the Jennesses, 'way back fifty
years or more. But that one never showed
itself; 'twas only a sort o' weepin' an'
groanin' an' complainin' noise goin' through
the house at night. An' they never encouraged it a mite, but sent for old Parson
Williams an' had him pray at it till it cleared
out. Then they aired the house thoroughly, an' never had a sign of it agin. But
here was I talkin' with one, 'sociatin' with
it, gettin' fond on it, an' really talkin' of
adoptin' it. What was I goin' to do? What
was I goin' not to do? Over an' over in my
mind I went at that, an' little sleep I got
that night, I tell you. As I said afore, we
was brought up in a pious fam'ly, an' my
religion, small 's it was to what it oughter
been, had brought me through all my
troubles so fur, as nothin' else could 'a'

done. So I prayed a good deal that night,
an' read my Bible lots. An' bimeby—'most
mornin' 'twas—I begun to git red o' that
whirlin', scaret kind o' thinkin', an' to look
at things stiddier an' easier. Mebbe 'twas
the prayin'; anyway I got all o' a suddin so
's to see the matter reasonable an' cipher it
out plain for myself. 'Twas about this way
I went at it. Fust place I says to myself:
"What's a ghost, anyway? Why, it's a
sperrit. An' what's a sperrit? Why, it's a
soul. Well, there ain't no harm in a soul;
we've all got 'em. But then," thinks I to
myself, "what's this soul doin' here?
Where's it been sence the boy died?" Well,
you see, I knowed too much about heaven,
from Scripter an' sermons an' all, to think
that a soul that once got there would leave
it to traipse round here agin an' speak
pieces. So I had to feel cert'in it hadn't
ever got to heaven 'tall. An' as for the
other place—why, you never, never in the
world, could 'a' made me b'lieve that Norvle
had been there. He wa'n't that kind, I
knowed. 'Twasn't jest because I'd got so
fond o' him, but I felt sure, sure, sure that
he'd never been there, in that awful suff'rin'
an' sin. He'd 'a' showed it if he had. Now
you see I was orth'dox, an' my folks afore

me, an' I'd never even heerd that any one thought there might be another place besides them two local'ties. Sence then I've read somewheres that there is sexes who b'lieve that, but I'd never heerd a hint of it then But seein' that he hadn't been to ary o' them two places, then where had he been, and why did he come to me? When I got to that p'int I had to stop short agin, an' havin' nothin' better to do, I went to prayin'. An' jest 's the mornin' light shone into my window there come a light shinin' right into my heart, an' I see it all. 'Twas this way. Norvle hadn't been fetched up by religious folks. For, strange 's it may seem, there's people like that, even in a Christian land. He'd been a well-meanin' boy, an' if he'd ever been learnt he'd 'a' took right hold o' religion, an' glad enough too. But he lived 'way off in the mountains, there wa'n't no meetin'-house within miles, an' his folks was like heathen. Even the deestrick school was too fur off for him to go, or else his pa wouldn't spare him to 'tend. So he'd growed up ign'runt of all he'd oughter know, never seein' a Bible, hearin' a sermon, or touchin' a cat'chism in all his life. He'd learnt how to read somehow, an' up in the garret he'd come acrost a book o' pieces sech as boys

speak to school. An' he'd took to 'em,
studied 'em, an' got so he could say 'em all.
But he had to do it all by hisself. Nobody
ever heerd him say 'em. Nobody would
listen when he tried to show off. That's
terr'ble hard on a boy. They like so to be
praised up an' noticed when they've done
anything. Why, Peleg, the youngest o' my
three boys, you know, allers set so by my
lookin' at his whittlin', or hearin' him sing,
or praisin' the pictur's he drawed on his
slate. But bimeby Norvle died; I don't
know how. I never was able to find that
out; whether 'twas o' sickness or an accident. But he died without ever havin' been
grounded in the right things. An'—oh, don't
you see it now? Don't you know what
come to me that early mornin', as I laid cryin' and prayin' in my bed there? He—I
mean *it*, Norvle's poor little ign'runt soul—
had been let to come to me; me that loved
boys and had lost 'em all. An' I was to be
the one to learn it what he hadn't never had
a chance to pick up afore he died. So I see
I needn't stop bein' fond o' it, but go on
lovin' it harder an' harder, till I'd loved it
right straight up into heaven, where it
would 'a' been now but for lack o' information.

I tell you that was a solemn day to me. I was happy one way, sorry another, an' I felt such a awful responsibility. I tell you 'tain't many that has seen a heft put on 'em as that. Jest think of it! the hull religious trainin' of a ghost! I was busy all day preparin' for it. I looked up all my books, the ones I used when I learnt the boys, an' the Sabbath-school ones. An' I made a kind o' plan how I was to begin, an' how long 'twould take to go through all the doctrines an' beliefs. Our folks was Congregationals, an though I wa'n't as set in my ways about my own Church as some be, still, as Norvle didn't seem to have any partikler leanin' to ary other belief, I meant to bring him up as I'd been brought. So o' course I had to begin with the fall, an' I studied on that 'most all day. As the time drawed nigh for the visit I was dreffle worked up. Seemed 's if I couldn't scasly bear it, to see the boy I'd got so attached to an' built so much on, an' know that he wa'n't a boy at all, but a ghost. I was settin' there, in my old seat by the window, an' for quite a spell arter the pepp-'mint scent come into the room I wouldn't turn my head. Fact is, I was cryin' so 't I could hardly see out of my eyes. But bimeby I looked round, an', jest 's I thought, there

it stood. My eyes was pretty wet, but I
winked out the water 's well 's I could. An'
's soon 's I could see its face plain, I knowed
that it knowed I knowed. It didn't have
that pleased, shinin' look in its eyes, but was
sort o' doubtful an' scary. It stepped slow
an' softly, as if it was goin' to stop every
step, an' when 'twas in front o' me, it said,
almost in a whisper, an' so mournful, "Don't
you want to hear me speak my piece?"

I brushed the water out o' my eyes an'
says, real hearty an' cordial, "Yes, deary,'
course I do."

He begun in sech a low, shaky voice :

"Here rests his head upon the lap of airth,
   A youth to fortin an' to fame unknown."

Poor little feller! I jest ached for him,
an' my throat felt all swelled up 's if I had
the quinsy. I made up my mind that minute
to give up the rest o' my days, if it took that
long, to savin' that little soul o' Norvle's.
An' he shouldn't never feel, if I could help
it, that I didn't exackly approve o' ghosts,
or thought a mite less o' him for bein' one.
Then I begun my religious teachin'. As I
said afore, my startin'-p'int was the fall.
But o' course I had to allude to the creation
fust. Adam an' Eve, an' all that. Then I

learnt him the verse out o' the New England Primer about "In Adam's fall," an' that led right up, you see, to 'riginal sin, nat'ral depravity, an' all that relates to them doctrines. I had to begin jest as you would with a baby, you see, right at the el'mentary things. Then I took the Westminster Shorter, an' learnt him from "man's chief end" to the decrees. 'Twas a short lesson, but I didn't want to tire him the fust time. He seemed real int'rested, an' I forgot for a minute he was a ghost, an' I says, "Norvle, s'pose you take this cat'chism home an'—" I stopped right off short, for I ree'lected he hadn't got any home, but was jest a wand'rin', ramblin', uneasy ghost. An' oh, where did he sleep nights? Thinkin' o' that made the tears come agin, an' I turned away to sop 'em up. When I looked round, it was gone.

You see I say "it" sometimes, an' then agin I say "him." I know I'd oughter say "it" all the time; but—well, 'way down in my old heart it's "him" an' "he" allers, an' he's no diff'ent from my other three boys.

I was a mite nervous next time. I wasn't quite cert'in I'd gone to work right with my lessons. I'd had some exper'ence teachin', what with my own boys an' a Sabbath-

school class. But how did I know but a
ghost's mind was all diff'ent, an' couldn't
take in the same things in the same way?
Then he didn't have no books, an' couldn't
look over the lesson at home. So mebbe—
I kep' sayin' to myself—he don't remember
a single word about Adam, or his sin, an'
the terr'ble consequences. But I needn't 'a'
worried; for I hadn't hardly time to answer
that same old question, "Don't you want to
hear me speak my piece?" afore he started
off:

> "Oh, what a fall was there, my conntrymen!
> Then me an' you an' all on us fell down."

Could a perfessor in the the'logical sem-
'nary 'a' put it better? The real cat'chism
doctrine, you see, "all maukind by the fall,"
an' so on. So I begun to feel encouraged.
This time I took foreord'nation an' election,
an' easy things like that. Eternal punishment goes along o' that lesson by rights, but
'twas sech a pers'nal subjeck for that poor
soul that I skipped it that once. So it went
on day arter day. I didn't allers keep to
the doctrines. I made 'lowances for Norvle's bringin' up, an' had more int'restin'
things now an' agin, like who was the fust
man, the strongest man, the meekest man,

an' them. An' seein' he was so fond o'
pieces, I learnt him pretty verses out o' the
New England Primer, like

> "Vashti for pride
> Was set aside,"

or'

> "Elijah hid,
> By ravens fed."

He was so tickled with that piece about

> "Good children must
> Fear God all day,
> Parents obey,
> No false thing say,"

an' so on. An' he liked about John Rog-
ers an' Agur's prayer, an' took right off to
that advice at the very eend o' the Primer,
by the late rev'rent an' ven'rable Mr. Na-
than'el Clap, o' Newport, on Rhode Island.

But the days was slippin' by, an' I begun
to worry. 'Twas September now, an' my
time was up early in October, for the fam'-
ly was comin' home then. An' go 's fast 's
I could I hadn't been able to git beyond
"the mis'ry o' that estate whereinto man
fell" in the cat'chism, an' the buildin' o'
the temple in the Bible. All about sin an'
punishment an' the old dispensation, you
see, an' never a speek of light an' hope for

that poor sperrit. For o' course I had to go
reg'lar an' take subjecks as they come, an'
didn't dast skip over into the New 'Test'-
ment comfort till its turn come. I was in a
heap o' trouble about it, when all of a suddin another chance was given me. Old Mr.
Rice come to me with a letter in his hand,
an' asked me if I couldn't be induced to stay
on an' take care o' the house through the
winter. Seems that one o' the children—
Mis' Davis's, I mean—had took cold, an' its
throat or lungs or something was weak. So
the doctor had ordered them to take her
'crost the water, an' they was goin' right off,
without comin' home at all. Wasn't it wonderful? A int'position o' Providence, cer-
t'in sure, an' I thanked the Lord on my bend-
ed knees. I kep' on now in the reg'lar way,
not havin' to hurry, givin' all the time I
wanted to the doctrines. For there's nothin' like bein' well grounded in them. Norvle never said much, but he showed plain
enough that he took 'em all in, by the ap-
proprit pieces he spoke arter each lesson. I
wish I could rec'lect 'em all; they was
wonderful. I know one time we had free-
will, an' 'twas the most excitin' occasion. I
got so worked up over it, showin' how 'twas
consistent with election an' foreord'nation,

an' argifyin' that wo was jest as free to pick
an' choose as—as—anybody. An' next time
he up an' speaks, " Hard, hard indeed was
the contest for freedom an' the struggle for
independence."

Oh, 'twas good as a sermon! An', agin,
arter a course o' lessons on the power o' the
devil an' how to resist him, he spoke that
powerful piece, " They tell us, sir, that wo
aro weak, unable to scope with so form'dable
a advers'ry; but when shall wo be stronger?" An' how he did go on about "Shall
wo 'quire the means o' effectooal resistance
by lyin' s'pinely on our backs an' huggin'
the d'lusive phantom o' hope?" an' all that.
One day I talked very strong about the Cath-
'lics, warned him ag'inst the Pope o' Rome,
an' forbid him ever to go near popish folks.
Next time he come he up an' spoke a piece
about

"Banished from Rome? What's banished but set -
free
From daily contracts?"

That showed his views about the Pope plain
enough, I think.

Oh, I never see a boy—let alone a ghost
—take in truths like him. An' it done me
good too. I'd got a little rusty on them

doctrinal b'liefs myself, an' it rubbed up my
knowledge wonderful. I studied up days,
an' could hardly wait for class-time to come;
an' jest 's soon 's I had the fust sniff o' pepp-
'mint arternoons, I'd be ready to start off.
But I'd allers give him his chance fust, an'
I growed to love that one thing he said every
time, the only thing I ever heerd him reely
say, "Don't you want to hear me speak my
piece?" It seemed to mean more an' more
each day, an' bimeby was 'most like a whole
conversation. Jest from that one remark I
begun to know all about his past life an' doin's, his folks, his home, an' all. A poor,
empty, neglected, lonesome life 'twas, an' my
heart ached over it as it come out day by
day in our talks. To think o' his never havin' had what my boys had so much on, all
their days; meetin's, Sabbath-schools, cat'-
chisms, preparat'ry lectur's, monthly concerts,
prayer-meetin's; he never 'd had one o' them
blessed priv'leges in his hull narrer little life.
Well, as I said, I enjoyed the doctrinal teachin', the Old Test'ment an' all; but I was
awful glad when with a clear conscience I
could turn over the leaf an' show him t'other side. He'd been gettin' rather low in his
mind lately, an' no wonder. For I hadn't
felt to tell him anything yet but about our.
12

dreflle state o' sin, the punishment we de-
served, an' the justice o' Him who could give
it to us. To be sure, I got him to the p'int
where he knowed 'twould be all perfectly
right, consid'rin' the circumstances, if he
should be sent right down to the place, as
the hymn says,

"Where crooked ways o' sinners lead."

He was resigned to it, but he wa'n't exackly
glad, an' he looked rather solemn. So I was
pleased enough when I begun to let in a
mite o' sunshinin' an' told him the gospel
story. An' I declare it never 'd meant so
much to me myself, church member as I'd
been for more'n a dozen years, as when I begun to tell it to that poor little ghost. I
begun 'way at the very beginnin', an' it was
quite a spell afore he see what was comin'.
He thought I was jest givin' an account of
a common, ord'nary boy. I see that was the
way to int'rest him, so I told about Him as
a little feller, with his mother, an' in the
carpenter's shop, an' round the water an'
the shore with the fishermen an' sailors. I
was thinkin' o' my own boys on the salt
water at Portsmouth an' Kitt'ry when I
dwelt so on that part. But pretty soon I
rec'lected how Norvle was fetched up on

risin' ground, so I told about His bein' so
fond o' the hills, goin' up "into a mountin
apart," as the Bible says, to pray an' to
preach, or to set there alone. An' how Norvle's face did light up then, an' his whity-
blue eyes shine! I don't doubt he was
thinkin' o' the New Hampshire hills. For
crampin' 's they be, folks that live among
'em do learn to love 'em lots. So it went
on, till it come nigh the last part o' the
narr'tive. No need for me to remind you o'
that. I'd knowed it allers, learnt it to my
Sabbath-school scholars, heerd it talked an'
preached an' sung all my born days, but
'twas like a bran'-new thing 's I told it to
Norvle, an' the tears jest ran down my face
like rain. He didn't cry. I guess ghosts
never does. But oh, how mournful an' sorry
he looked, with his eyes opened wide an'
lookin' straight into my face, an' his lips
kind o' tremblin'! For quite a spell now
he'd been speakin' diff'ent sort o' pieces —
hymns an' sech. An' now he begun to say
sech beautiful ones, hymns an' psalms I
hadn't even thought on for years. Some o'
'em I learnt afore I could read, from hearin'
mother say 'em over 'n' over to me as I set
on the little cricket at her feet. How I felt
as he'd say, soft an' gentle like, "Don't you

want to hear me speak my piece ?" an' then
foller it right up with one o' them sweet old
hymns I always rec'lected in mother's voice!
Oh, I loved him harder 'n' harder every day!
He was jest 's homely 's ever, jest 's freckled,
his hair jest 's reddish-yeller an' mussy, but
he looked diff'ent, somehow. There was a
kind o' rested, quiet, satisfied look come on
his face by spells that made him prettier to
look at. An' bimeby that look come to stay.
I couldn't make you understand 'f I tried—
an' I ain't goin' to try—how I see what was
happenin' in that soul. But I did see. I
knowed the very hour—the minute 'most—
when he see the hull truth an' give up to it.
There didn't seem to be any powerful conviction o' sin. Mebbe ghosts don't need to
go through that. P'r'aps it's their bodies
that makes that work so strong in folks, an'
ghosts 'ain't got any bodies. So 'twas a
easy, smooth specie o' conversion, an' Norvle
hisself didn't seem to know when it happened. He kep' comin' jest the same, allers
askin' his little question, an' speakin' his
piece. An' allers there come with him that
pepp'minty scent. To this day that common, ev'ry-day, physicky smell brings more
things back to me than even cinnamon-roses
or day-lilies like them in the old garden on

the Odiorne's P'int road. I went on all the
time with my teachin'. I knowed Norvle
was all right now, an' safe for ever 'n' ever.
But there's plenty o' things even perfessors
need to know, an' I did so like to learn him.

"Twas gettin' past the middle o' December
now. One day I walked a little ways down
street for exercise an' fresh air, an' all to
once there come over me sech a strong rec'-
lection o' Portsmouth woods. I didn't know
why 'twas for a minute, but then I begun to
smell a piny, woodsy smell, an' I see right
on the sidewalk a lot o' evergreens — pine
an' hemlock an' spruce. Then I remembered
that Christmas was comin'. You see, pa an'
ma had allers made a good deal o' Christmas. Congregationals in old times never
done so. I know pa said that one time old
Parson Pickerin', o' Greenland, sent back a
turkey that gran'f'ther Jenness give him
Christmas, sayin' he'd ruther have it some
other time than on a popish hollerday. But
we was fetched up to keep the day. Why,
up to the very last Christmas o' their lives
my three boys hung their blue-yarn stockin's
up by the fireplace, though Amos was past
nineteen then, an' Ezry goin' on seventeen.
So 'twas a time full o' rec'lectin' for me.
The year afore I'd jest put it all out o' my

head an' tried to forget what day 'twas.
But I couldn't forget it here. 'Twas in the
air; 'twas ev'rywhere you went. The stores
was full o' playthings, folks was traipsin'
through the streets with their hands an'
arms full o' bundles, ev'rybody that passed
you was talkin' about it, an' 'twas no use
tryin' to git red on it. It made me choky
an' wat'ry-eyed all the time, an' I couldn't
see nothin' ary blessed minute but the old
wood fire at home, with the big yarn stockin's hangin' there. But one day arter Norvle had left, an' the pepp'mint scent hadn't
quite gone out o' the room, I begun to think
why I couldn't make a Christmas for him.
Now don't laugh at me. I wa'n't a fool. I
knowed 's well 's you do that ghosts don't
want presents or keep days. But I was so
lonesome, an' jest hungry for a stockin' to
fill—a boy's stockin'. "So why," I says to
myself, "shouldn't I make b'lieve—'play,'
's the children says—that Norvle wants a
real old-fashioned Christmas, an' I can give
him one?" The next time he come I led
up to the subject an' found out, 's I suspi-
cioned, that he'd never heerd o' Christmas
or Santy Claus in all his born days. So I
told him all about it, an' he was so int'rested. Fust I told him whose birthday 'twas,

o' course, an' why folks kep' it. Then I told
him about fam'lies all gettin' together at
that time, an' comin' home from every-
wheres, to be with their own folks. An' I
went on about hangin' up stockin's an' fillin'
'em with presents. "An' now, Norvle," I
says, "I'm goin' to make a real old-fashioned
Christmas for you this year, sech as we used
to have in the old house; sech as we made
for Amos an' Ezry an' Peleg. For," I says,
"you've been a real good boy this winter,
an' I set as much by you 'most—p'r'aps jest
as much—as I done by my own boys." He
looked dreffle tickled, an' so 'twas settled.
How I did enjoy gettin' ready! 'Twa'n't so
easy as it seems. For I'd set my heart on
havin' the same kind o' presents as we used
to give the boys, an' they wa'n't plenty
in New York City. The stockin' was easy
enough, for I had one o' Peleg's. You see,
I kind o' liked to have some o' the boys'
things about, an' I had some o' the old blue
feetin' layin' on my stockin' basket 's if they
was waitin' to be darned. They looked nat'-
ral an' good, you see. Peleg was nigh about
Norvle's size. Then I wanted a partikler
specie o' apple, big an' red an' shiny; we
called 'em the Boardman reds. I found some
to the market at last. They didn't exackly

look like the old kind; but the man said
they was, he'd jest fetched 'em from Portsmouth hisself. The hick'ry-nuts I got easy
enough, an' the maple sugar. I was goin'
to get some pepp'mint lozengers, for my boys
all thought so much o' them, but it seemed
too pers'nal, an' I give 'em up. I got a big
stick o' ball lick'rish, though — boys allers
like that—an' some B'gundy pitch to chew.
Then o' course there must be a jack-knife.
I found jest the right kind, big, with a black
horn handle an' two blades. I set up late
nights an' riz early to knit a pair o' red-yarn
mittens, like Peleg's; they're so good for
snowballin', you know. An' I wound a yarn
ball, an' covered it with leather. I had a
diff'cult time findin' the fish-hooks an' sink-
ers, for I hadn't been round no great in New
York, an' there ain't no general store there.
But I found 'em at last. Right on top I was
going to put Pely's little chunky, leather-
cover Bible. Mother give it to him the day
he jined the church, an' writ his name in her
straight up an' down prim handwritin'. I
knowed she an' him both would be willin'
it should go to this poor little soul the
Scripters meant so much to, an' had done so
much for.

The New York greens didn't satisfy me.

There was some stuff with sicky green leaves an' white, tallery-lookin' berries, an' some all shinin' an' pricky, with red fruit. But they didn't look nat'ral. Bimeby I come acrost some ground-pine, sech as growed all through the wood lot behind the old house, spranglin' over the ground, an' some juniper, like what spread amongst the rocks there, with its little black berries an' sharp, scratchy needles. I couldn't get any black alder nor bittersweet berries, an' had to do without 'em. Oh, you don't know what it was to me, an' my poor empty heart that had ached till 'twas 'most numb, to get that stockin' ready. Ev'ry day I talked Christmas to Norvle, never lettin' him know, o' course, what I was goin' to give him, but tellin' all about diff'rent Christmases I'd knowed. I went on about how the fam'ly was allers together, an' father wore his best clothes an' set to the head o' the table, an' mother t'other end, an' me an' the boys all there. 'Twas nat'ral, I s'pose, consid'rin' that I dwelt on that part on it, folks all bein' together that day, lovin' an' doin' for their very own. Then I told him how Christmas Eve we all used to stand together, the boys an' me, afore we went to bed, an' sing pa's favrit piece, " Home, Sweet Home." I carried the toon, Peleg sung a real sweet second, Ezry had the high part, an' Amos the low. How it fetched it all back to tell it over to him!.

The last night but one come—the twenty-third 'twas. Norvie had looked real mournful-like lately. Ev'ry time I spoke o' father's house, or fam'lies gettin' together or goin' home for Christmas, I see he looked kind o' sorry an' 's if he wanted somethin'. But I wouldn't see what it meant. That arternoon, though, when he'd ast, in a shaky, still voice, "Don't you want to hear me speak my piece?" he follered it up with the dear old hymn mother whispered part of the very last day of her life—

"Airth has engrossed my love too long,
    'Tis time to lift my eyes."

He went on with all the verses, an' when he come to

"O let me mount to join their song,"

he said it 's if he was prayin' to me, an' seech a longin' sound come into his voice, an' such a longin' look into his eyes, that I was all goose-flesh, an' so choky. When he'd finished, I turned away to get my handk'chief, an' when I looked back agin he was gone.

Well, I s'pose you see now what I'd got to
do, and what my plain duty was. I really
had knowed it all along, but I'd shet my
eyes to it a purpose till now ; but I couldn't
no longer. That poor soul o' Norvle's was
regen'rated, saved cert'in sure, an' what
business had I got-to keep it down here any
longer ? You see it plain enough, but no
one but me — an' One other — knows how
much it meant to me that night. "Couldn't
I," says I to myself—"couldn't I keep him
only one day longer, jest over that seas'n o'
Christmas, so hard, so ter'ble hard to bear
without him ? Anyway, couldn't I have him
till mornin', an' let him have his stockin' ?
When he was goin' to have sech a long, long
time up there, would jest one day more down
here make any great diff'rence ?" The answer come quick enough. "Yes, 'twould !
He b'longed somewher's else, an' I must send
him there, an' right straight off, too, even if
it broke my heart all to pieces doin' it."

All the next day I went about my work
very softly. It seemed like the day o' the
boy's fun'ral. I'd filled the stockin' two
days afore—I couldn't wait—an' there it
laid in my room, never, never, to be hung
up, all bulgy an' onreg'lar an' knobby. I
knowed what ary bulge meant. That one

by the ankle was the jack-knife, an' that queer place nigh the knee was where the stick o' lick'rish had got crosswise an' poked 'way out each side. There was one Board- man red apple roundin' out the toe like a darnin' ball, an' right in the top was Pely's chunky little Bible jest showin' above the ribbed part. I didn't empty it. Folks will keep sech things, you know, an' it's up in my bedroom somewher's now, I b'lieve.

Well, Christmas Eve come, an' come quick —too quick for me that time. I'd made up my mind 'twouldn't never do to let Norvle see how I felt. I had a good deal o' Jenness grit, an' I called it all up now. So, when he come in, I was jest as usual, an' smiled at him real pleasant; but I felt 'twouldn't do to wait a single minute, for fear I'd break down, so afore he could make his one little remark, for the fust time since I knowed him, I begun fust, an' he stood still an' listened.

"Norvle," I says, speakin' 's I used to to the boys' playfellers that used to come an' see 'em an' want to stay on an' on—"Norvle, I've had a real nice visit with you. I've enjoyed your comp'ny lots, an' I wish I could ask you to stay longer. But it's Christmas Eve, you know, an', 's I've often told you,

people 'd oughter be with their own folks
to-night. You know now where your folks
is, leastways your Father an' your Elder
Brother. So, I'm dreffle sorry to seem im-
perlite an' send you off, but—why, this bein'
Christmas Eve, 's I says afore, I really think
—the best thing for you to do—is—to go—
Home!" I got it out somehow; I don't see
how I done it.

Norvle looked right at me, kind o' mourn-
fle. He stood stock-still, an' I thought he
was goin' to make his one little remark,
but he didn't. Jest 's true 's I live, that boy
opened his mouth an' begun to sing. An'
oh! what do you suppose he sung? "Home,
Sweet Home!" He'd never sung afore: I
didn't know 's he could; but his voice was
like a wood-robin now. An' in a minute,
though there wa'n't anybody but him an'
me in the room, seemed 's if I heerd some
other voices. Norvle carried the toon, but
I heerd a real sweet second, an' then a high
part an' a low. 'Twas jest like four boys
singin' together. An' while I looked at him
the music sounded further 'n' further off, till
when he got to the last "sweet—sweet—
home," I had to lean 'way forward to ketch
a sound. An' when it stopped — why, he
stopped. He didn't go; he jest wasn't there.

Well, I've got along somehow. You do
get along through most things, hard 's they
be. It's more 'n forty year now sence my
ghost story happened, an' I'm an old woman.
I'm failin' lately pretty fast, an' it makes
me think a good deal about goin' home myself to jine pa 'n' ma 'n' the boys. I might
's well tell you that when I say the boys, I
mean *four* on 'em. For, b'sides my three,
I'm cert'in there's goin' to be another one, a
little chap with rough, reddish-yeller hair,
an' lots o' freckles. Course I know it's all
diff'ent up there, an' things ain't a speck like
what they be here; but somehow it won't
seem exackly nat'ral if that little feller don't
somewher's in the course o' conv'sation bring
in that favrit remark o' his'n,

"Don't you want to hear me speak my
piece?"

MONSIEUR ALCIBIADE.

BY CONSTANCE CARY HARRISON.

A TRANSPARENTLY gentle despot, who might have been led by the finger-tip of the youngest member of his class, was M. Alcibiade de St. Pierre, the Belhaven dancing-master, who gave also lessons in his native tongue. Nature had endowed him with a stationary scowl, his moustaches curled wildly, and he bore upon the brow a cicatrix that caused his pupils to liken him to the swashbuckler heroes of Dumas, Scott, or Cervantes. In outward appearance he was Aramis, Athos, Porthos, and D'Artagnan in one, with a dash of Le Balafré and Don Quixote thrown in.

Although this picturesque personage was a comparative new-comer in the town, the forebear of M. Alcibiade had arrived in America as pendant to an expedition supplying an interesting chapter of colonial

history. Early in the spring of 1790 came
into port at Belhaven a party of French
immigrants engaged by Playfair, an English
agent, and De Soissons, a nimble-tongued
deceiver of his compatriots, in behalf of an
enterprise organized in New England, and
styled the Ohio Land Company, to people
the wilderness near the mouth of the Ka-
nawha River, beyond the western woods of
Virginia. Among the travellers, whose weary
hearts beat high with hope as they touched
the shore of a fancied El Dorado, were men
skilled in the exquisite handicrafts of a per-
fected civilization. Carvers there were of
furniture like wooden lace-work; beaters of
fine brass fashioned into *rocaille* decorations;
painters of shepherds piping to their fair,
of Cupids turning somersaults in chains of
roses; harpsichord-tuners; makers of gild-
ed carriages; varnishers of panels that
shone like mirrors; disciples of Boule and
Martin; confectioners; perruquiers — and
all, by a fine irony of fate, bound for a log-
hut settlement, where the cry of savage
beasts, or the war-whoop of the deadly Indian, was to be their nightly lullaby.

What eloquence had prevailed upon these
hapless beings to believe they were to be
the founders of a brave new Paris in the

Western Hemisphere, their wily managers
alone could tell. The first instalment of
the five hundred Frenchmen said to have
been thus deluded, numbering with their
wives and children about sixty, after much
waiting at Belhaven, their souls within them
vexed by homesickness and hope deferred,
split up into variously minded factions.
Some pressed on, under charge of a long-
delayed messenger of the company, to the
frontier; others put their all into a return
passage to France; and a few elected to
remain and try their fortunes in the little
town which in those days had no end of am-
bitious projects for future greatness.

One of these prudent ones was a gay old
bachelor, Alcibiade St. Pierre, self-styled
" Hair-dresser to the Court of France." He
opened a snug little shop, where the gentry
of town and country dropped in to have
their perukes dressed and tied, to be shorn,
perfumed, and shampooed, after the latest
fashions in vogue before Alcibiade had set
sail for the New World. He was sometimes
sent for to bleed, or to apply leeches, and
his *mille-fleurs* graces impressed the towns-
people mightily. As his trade increased,
Alcibiade was called on to lament the sad
fortunes of his fellow-immigrants. Most of

13

those who became frontiersmen had suc-
cumbed to want and hardships, had met the
horrors of Indian massacre, or had gone
under in the collapse of an international
speculation that carried down its promoters
in the crash. From those who returned to
France had come dolorous accounts of com-
motion in their beloved capital. Decidedly,
thought M. Alcibiade, it were better to stag-
nate in Belhaven than be forced by a mob
in Paris to dress the head of some former
patron upon a pike!

Simple-minded, kindly, cheery as *le petit
homme gris*, the little hair-dresser became a
great favorite. A trig Scotch lassie, daughter
of a settler, having fallen in love with him,
the father consented to the match on condition that the intended son-in-law would
renounce his French patronymic and trans-
late himself into plain "A. Peters" upon his
sign and in his official signature. And thus
it came to pass that, instead of the stylish
frontispiece so flattering to town pride, there
arose above the shop door an announcement
remaining there until its blue and gold were
dimmed by time,

A. PETERS,

LADIES' AND GENTS' HAIR-DRESSER

AND BARBER.

And, farther down,

WIGS AND TOUPETS.

DISEASES OF THE SCALP.

ONGUENTS AND SCENTS.

HAIR-POWDER, ROUGE, AND PATCHES.

ATTENDANCE AT HOUSE FOR BALLS AND
ROUTS.

Also,

TEETH PULLED, AND LIVELY LEECHES
CONSTANTLY IN STOCK.

By the smiles and blushes of his buxom
bride the gallant Alcibiade considered himself well paid for his self-sacrifice. Con-
tinuing to prosper, he gave hostages to hair-
dressing in the shape of several little lads
who spoke English with a broad Scotch burr,
French not at all, and, later in life, seized
with nostalgia, emigrated with his family to
end his days on the soil that gave him
birth.

Old Mr. Peters had become a figment of
tradition in the town when his grandson, the
present Alcibiade, appeared upon the scene.
To the ancestral St. Pierre the new representative had prefixed a patrician "de,"
vaguely explained as having been resumed

by the family on recovering possession of estates lost in the French Revolution. To plain people in Belhaven this prefix was interpreted to be an initial letter D, doing duty for a middle name not given. As for the estates, they must have been limited to the amount aptly if not elegantly designated by the French Commandant Marin in the conference with the Half-King of the Six Nations, recorded by Washington in 1753, when he said, "Child, you talk foolish; there is not so much land as the black of my nail yours."

When first arrived in Belhaven, the poor Frenchman was indeed in a pitiable plight. The attention of the town was called to him by certain readings and recitations in his own language, advertised to be given in Lafayette Hall.

Gay Berkeley, who, with her maiden aunt Penelope, had gone into Mrs. Dibble's shop to purchase pens and writing-paper, picked up from the counter a document in manuscript that excited her amused curiosity. It was apparently a programme, written on foolscap in a fine copperplate hand, and expressed in a queer French-English that would have been a credit to the manual known to fame as the "Portuguese Grammar and Guide to Polite Conversation."

"On my arrival from the France, me Alcibiade de St. Pierre, Chevalier of the Legion
of Honor and ex-artist of the theaters of
Paris, do make hurry to throw myself at the
feet of illustrious citizens of Belhaven, with
a presentment special of selections from the
immortal Racine et Corneille, such presentment to have place Hall Lafayette, the Monday evening to follow. Receive, ladies and
gentlemen, my distinguished hommages and
impressed salutations your very humble ser-
viteur."

" What in the world is this, Mrs. Dibble?"
asked the young lady, with dimpling cheeks.

" Indeed, Miss Gay, I told the chevalier
that it wouldn't be long catchin' the eye o'
my best customers," responded Mrs. Dibble,
complacently. " I helped him out a bit with
the words he didn't know. Dear heart, if it
wasn't only but for the handwritin', as good
as Mr. Johnson's nephew that was put in
state's prison for forgery, pore fellow, he
that used to practise here with fine nibs an'
broad nibs, writin' cards—spread eagles with
your name in curlicues comin' out o' their
beaks—an' true-lovers' knots an' doves, if 't
was a new-married pair. Miss Penelope,
I'm ashamed to say I'm clean out o' quills;

but old Farmer Berry up at the cross-roads,
the only one I can trust to pick the geese
properly, 'll bring me a new lot to-morrow.
Miss Gay, now, she's new school, 'n uses
steel—sand, ma'am? Yes; of course. The
usual quantity? Here's sweet note-paper,
Miss Gay, just received from Baltimore, the
tip o' the mode, they say — pale pink an'
skim-milk blue. Plain white, did you say,
miss? Yes; I've some cream-laid, like
you've always used befo'. If you're nothin'
better to do, ladies, 'twould be a charity
to that pore Mounseer to patronize his performance a Monday night. If 'twas only
for old times' sake, Miss Penelope, ma'am;
many's the head he's dressed—I mean his
grandfather's dressed—for your fam'ly. Yes;
old Mr. Peters's grandson, as I'm alive,
ma'am, an' the entertainment most genteel.
Selections from Corneel an' Raycine; fifty
cents for adults, twenty-five for children,
an' a special reduction for ladies' schools.
I thought there'd be a chance to get the
young gentlemen from Mr. Penhallow's Acad-
emy; but the chevalier kinder shrivelled
up at the mention o' boys, an' said 'twas
too hard to keep up the true dignity o'
the drama when they was present—Lord
knows, since I took to keepin' sweet stuff in

t'other winder, I'm up to the ways o' boys. If it's only a penny horse-cake—comin' back as bold as brass, with the hind-legs eat off, declarin' they's found a dead fly instead o' a currant for the eye, an' wantin' their money or another cake—"

"Do take some tickets, Aunt Pen," pleaded Gay.

"You know my sister does not approve of anything theatrical, my love," whispered Aunt Penelope. "Most of our church-members think with her. To be sure dear mamma used often to tell us of the time when General Washington and his lady, and Miss and Master Custis, drove up to stop two nights at grandpapa's, expressly to attend 'The Tragedy of Douglas,' by Mr. Home, and a play called 'The Inconstant; or, The Way to Win Him.' Mamma saw all the entertainments of the kind, I believe. It was thought of differently in those days."

"Doctor Falconer," ventured Gay, mentioning an eminent divine, "quoted, when he last drank tea with us, a passage from Racine. And these are only recitations, auntie, no acting or costumes."

"Oh, in that case," said Aunt Penelope, taking out her purse, "you may give me four tickets, Mrs. Dibble, and you may in-

vite two members of your French class,
child. Seats in the second row, if you
please, Mrs. Dibble. In a thing of this kind
it is well to be near enough to study the expression of the performer's face; and one
likes to forget the crowd when it's poetry.
I'm sure sister Finetta will be pleased to hear
about old Mr. Peters's grandson."

Lafayette Hall was a dingy, ill-lighted
room over the second floor of the building
in which Mrs. Dibble kept her shop. To the
young people it was associated with the in-
termittent delights of performances with
trained dogs and canaries; by Blind Tom,
a negro pianist who could repeat every air
suggested to him by the audience, and play
better with his hands behind him than most
of his hearers in the natural attitude; by
the tuneful Hutchinson family, who stood in
a row and warbled; by jugglers always interesting, and returned missionaries less al-
luring to the young; of May exhibitions of
female seminaries, whereat the pupils in book-
muslin with arbor-vitæ wreaths recited before applauding parents poems in honor of
their queen, and were afterwards regaled
with lemonade and cake. It was there that
Gay, as first lady-in-waiting, had once re-
tired behind the queen's throne in tears,

because her majesty had not scrupled to
twit her with wearing one of Aunt Pen's
muslins " made over "—which was too true.

Even now Gay could not divest herself of
the exhilaration produced by the sight of
that green baize curtain and the oil-lamps
serving as footlights. When, on the evening
of the chevalier's début, she came into the
hall, she nodded on every side to her friends,
with a feeling that this was life. Mrs. Dibble, whose person was attired in grass-green
mousseline de laine, with a wide collar of
dotted net, trimmed with cotton lace, took
tickets at the door; and in a conspicuously
good seat sat Viney Piper, the little day-
dressmaker, whose passion for the drama led
her to patronize every respectable show that
came to town. Viney had arrived upon the
opening of the doors at six o'clock, and the
performance was advertised to begin at
half-past seven. She was an odd-looking,
albino sort of creature, with pinkish eyes
and eyelids, pale flaxen hair, and a hook-
nose much to one side of her face. The
chevalier, entering the hall, had caught
sight of her on his way to the rear of the
stage, and forthwith executed a sweeping
bow that Viney thought the perfection of
foreign elegance.

When the hall was fairly filled, and the shuffling of feet announced the right degree of impatience on the part of the audience, the curtain, pulled up by the performer himself, rose upon a stage empty save for a small pine table displaying a white china water-pitcher and a goblet. M. Alcibiade, wearing a suit of rusty black, with a scarlet-satin stock and white-kid gloves, an order in his button-hole, his hair fiercely ruffled, and his eyes gleaming at some foe unknown, holding a dinner-knife in his clinched hand, stalked on the scene. At this alarming apparition a little girl sitting by her mamma burst into tears, and had to be consoled with gum-drops from the parental pocket, interspersed with audible assurances that the gentleman meant no harm. Opening his lips, Alcibiade poured forth a cataract of words, of which the most advanced French scholars in Miss Meechin's senior class could make neither head nor tail. He raved, he roared, he ranted; then seizing a goblet from the table, half filled it with water, and, holding the dagger in his other hand, advanced to the footlights calling on Heaven to end his woes. At last, drinking the contents of the poisoned cup, he threw away the dinner-knife, and fell with a gurgling

groan and a crash that made the lamps rattle in the chandelier. This, by agreement
with Mrs. Dibble, was the signal for that
worthy lady to hurry behind the scenes and
let fall the curtain on the direful sight; but
she, unfortunately, stood like a stock, aver-
ring afterwards that her blood was "that
cruddled with awr she couldn't 'a' budged
a mite!" Next, M. Alcibiade, coming slowly
back to life, sat up to confront the audience
with a smile of absolute fatuity; then
scrambling to his feet, bowed, kissed his
hand, and, going off, let the green baize descend on act the first.

It was long since Belhaven had enjoyed
such a merry spectacle. The school-girls
leading off with infectious giggles, every
bench caught the contagion, and only Viney
Piper, mopping real tears from her eyes, announced herself a connoisseur of true art.

The rest of the programme, although less
explosive, met with hysterically suppressed
mirth. Before its close, indeed, the audience had filtered slowly from the hall, leaving only the faithful Viney and Mrs. Dibble,
the newspaper-carrier (who was stone-deaf),
a scrub-woman with her baby in arms, and
a few citizens who exacted their money's
worth.

It was evident that provincial taste had not been educated to the dramatic standard of old Mr. Peters's grandson. Alcibiade, failing in other occupations, sank from poverty to want. One day when Miss Vincy Piper, arriving at the Berkeleys' house in Princess Royal Street, had established herself in the sewing-room, the ladies in submissive attitudes before her, the little dressmaker could hardly wait to dispose of business before introducing the subject near her heart.

"Just keep on running up them skirt-widths, Miss Gay ; an' Miss Penelope, ma'am, you could be gofferin' that sleeve while I get the body ready to try on," she said, marshalling her forces like a general in command. "Did you hear the news—that old Mr. Peters's grandson ain't expected to live the day out ? Fairly starved, I reckon, 'fore he'd let Mrs. Dibble know, an' he sleepin' in a hole of an attic at the Drovers' Hotel—kinder low fever, nothin' catchin', the doctor says, but nothin' to bring him up again. Such a beautiful genius he is, ma'am, an' a temper like a child, for all he looks so fierce."

"Starving! What do you mean, Vincy ?" said Miss Penelope, excitedly. "Go, Gay, fetch me my bonnet and mantilla, and help

Susan to pack a basket with some things. How comes it that nobody knew ?"

" It's all right for the present, Miss Penelope, ma'am," said Viney, blushing. "That's what's kep' me a little late this mornin'. I took up a few trifles, an' Mrs. Dibble she's got somebody to mind the store, and is to stay with him all day. But if you'd let Peggy put on a chicken to boil down for jelly, it wouldn't be wasted if—" here she swallowed once or twice and stabbed her pin-cushion — "if the pore Mounseer can't make no use of it."

The "pore Mounseer," however, surviving the day under Mrs. Dibble's kindly care, and finding no lack of nourishment during the days that followed, was, with the assistance of a subscription among some charitable people, transferred in the course of a week to a spare room let to single gentlemen by Mrs. Piper, Viney's mother, which by happy accident had been recently vacated.

The Pipers lived in one of the small frame-houses built to open directly upon the moss-encircled bricks set diagonally in the ancient sidewalk of a modest street. Their door-stone of white marble was accounted in the neighborhood a badge of distinguishing elegance, as was also a small brass oval serving

as a bell-pull, when most people used knock-
ers, or "knuckles," the gossips would aver.
The late Mr. Piper had been a seafaring
man, and had risen to be first mate of the
brig *Polly and Nancy,* when, on a return
voyage from Cadiz with a cargo of fruit,
salt, and wines, bound for Belhaven port, he
was swept overboard in a hurricane and lost.

The best room of the little house, into
which one stepped out of the street direct,
was a sort of marine museum like a chill
grotto, suggesting a mermaid's clutch or the
grip of shark's teeth. Here Mrs. Piper did
not care to raise the shades, except at one
side window permanently darkened by a
trellis overgrown with a vine of the Isabella
grape. The children of Miss Viney's customers liked to be sent to make appointments
with that busy little body ; for Mrs. Piper,
too deaf to answer questions, and droning
her explanations in a sing-song voice, always
showed them around the museum with great
affability. The old woman usually sat in a
clean kitchen opening upon the back yard,
where, under the damson-trees and amid the
hundred-leaf rose-bushes, were constructed
little winding walks, edged with shells, and
leading up to seats made of a whale's back-
bone.

After the Chevalier de St. Pierre had suc-
ceeded in obtaining classes in dancing and
deportment that enabled him to live, and
had settled down to become a fixture in the
widow's house, his spare moments were
given to cultivating flowers in the beds between the shell-bordered walks. Everything
grows easily in soft Belhaven air, and soon
the Pipers' garden became a proverb in the
place. Mrs. Piper's only complaint against
her lodger was couched in the expressive
phrase, "The Lord knows how often he
empties his water-jug"; but even a distaste
for ablution yielded in time to the insistent
cleanliness of his surroundings. Sometimes,
to cheer "Madame Pipère" in her solitude,
Alcibiade would descend to the kitchen and
proffer to the old woman, knitting in her
sunny window-seat, "a leetle divertissement
from ze classique drama of La France." He
had a *vrai* inspiration for the stage, St.
Pierre confessed to Viney, and but for political intrigue would be now in his rightful
place on the boards of the Théâtre Français.
These exhibitions, repeating the celebrated
performance of his début at Lafayette Hall,
were as deeply and religiously admired by
the widow as by her daughter.

One day occurred a variant upon the

usual exercise. Alcibiade had always treated poor lank Viney as if she were one of the great ladies of the court in bondage to his ancestor's curling-tongs; but she was unprepared for the scene that greeted her return when, having stepped down to Slater's for a spool of "forty" cotton, she found the chevalier, in his best black suit, wearing white kid gloves, and holding a bouquet in one hand, kneeling at Mrs. Piper's feet and kissing her finger-tips with reverence.

"I ask you, madame, for the hand of your beautiful and admirable child in marriage," was what Viney and the whole neigborhood within ear-shot heard him roar.

Viney, with all her good qualities, was a bit of a virago. The absurdity of the proceeding, and the sense that her adjacent acquaintances were laughing at her affairs, flooded her thin skin with blushes and her soul with anger. While Mrs. Piper, scared out of her wits, was about to open her.lips for a feeble screech, Viney whisked into the kitchen, snatched Alcibiade's bouquet, threw it away into a parsley-bed, and boxed the professor's ears.

"You'd better believe I give 'im a piece of my mind," she narrated afterwards to Miss Penelope and Gay. "But, bless you, he

cried so pitiful, an' begged our pardons so
kind o' honorable, I had not the heart to
turn him out o' the house like I threatened
to. Them white kids, Miss Gay! An' at
his age, an' mine! The notion's too cryin'
ridic'lous." And she snapped a seam into
the beak of her sewing-bird with vicious
emphasis, giving at the same time a sidelong
glance into the mirror, and a complacent
toss of the head.

No one could be long in the chevalier's
company without discovering that a very
dove of gentleness and affectionate gratitude
dwelt in his gaunt envelope of flesh. So, re-
straining his pretensions as a lover, he
meekly accepted Miss Viney's fiat, and went
about the town looking as warlike as ever,
but inwardly carrying a broken spirit. One
of his dancing-class encountered him crossing a windy common in the suburbs of the
town pursued by a flock of geese, from whose
sibilant obloquy he was making nervous
efforts to escape; and it was known to the
boys and girls that the chevalier was always alarmed by the apparition of a spider
or a cow. No wonder the young people decided that Alcibiade had been reduced to
pulp by Miss Viney's vigorous rejection of
his suit. The little dress-maker's peppery

14

temper was familiar to the offspring of her customers, from whom she would stand no trifling around her temporary throne in their respective households.

When the war between the States broke out, Viney seemed to have found her destined vocation as a red-hot secessionist. Not very clear, fundamentally, as to what she resented on the part of the national authorities at the other end of the Long Bridge, some eight miles away, she threw out her rebel banner on the wall, sang "Dixie" in her shrill treble, declaimed, protested, and, in short, kept everybody in her vicinity in a boiling state of excitement about the condition of political affairs. When the Belhaven regiments went on to Richmond or Manassas, Viney stitched her fingers to the bone making shirts for them, while Mrs. Piper knit socks of gray wool as fast as her needles could fly. They also turned out a number of the white linen havelocks and gaiters adopted by one of the companies and afterward discarded as a too shining mark for opposing riflemen. Viney trotted to the train to see the boys go off, and stood there in the crowd, cheering and waving with the best. As she watched the last car recede on two gleaming lines of steel, its rear platform thronged with gesticulating shapes in gray, she felt her heart inflate and her stature grow with a yearning desire to go out and fight or do something helpful in their ranks.

When she turned to walk home that afternoon of balmy spring, there, haunting her footsteps, was the faithful Alcibiade. He looked into her watery blue eyes as if imploring to be allowed to speak his sympathy.

"Have it out, an' be done with it, for gracious' sake," said Viney, pettishly. His smooth-finished black coat, his waxed moustache, the bunch of jonquils in his buttonhole, fretted her beyond endurance.

"Those tears for the brave, they are a benison," said Alcibiade, sentimentally. "Who would not be inspired by them to deeds of glory?"

"It's not the boys I'm cryin' for," said Viney. "It's us that are left behind and have got to put our necks under the vandal's heel." That "vandal" afforded a famous outlet for secession wrath in those days; it may be doubted whether the war could have been carried on without him. "Oh! if 't worn't for mother, d'ye think I'd stay? I'd go to-morrow, an' carry a water-pail to fill canteens; or I'd nurse in hospitals—or anything."

"It's a noble, a sacred cause," replied the chevalier, looking down at the toe of his varnished boot to avoid the needle-point of her eye. "You will permit me, *chère* Mees Viney, to mingle with yours my prayers for its success? When I think that this Virginia that has sheltered two exiles of our house — my ancestor, who came here to find a home, a bride, a thousand friends, a thousand tendernesses; and me, less fortunate, but ever grateful for the hour that brought you, an angel of goodness, to my rescue in distress—"

"That's neither here nor there," interrupted Viney, cruelly. "Besides, it was as much Mrs. Dibble as me, anyway."

"But you will not deny me the privilege of sharing your patriotic anxiety for the welfare of the troops? You will allow my heart to beat in unison with yours?"

"Nobody ain't a-preventin' your heart doin' what it pleases," said the uncompromising lady of his love, now fairly out of patience with his phrasing. "But it's deeds, not words, that show what a man's worth nowadays. When I think what a fool I used to be 'bout fine talkin', an' how I be-

lieved if a feller spread himself in speechi-
fyin' he was boun' to be a hero, it makes me
fairly sick. I'd rather have the little finger
o' one o' them privates that's in the train
we hear whistlin' up yonder — bless their
souls! — than the whole body of a dandy
Jim that stays at home. But, law me. I'm
foolish talkin' such stuff to *you*."

Foolish and manifestly unjust, we will
agree with her. But Viney's seed was not
sown on barren soil, as we shall see. From
that date the chevalier's moustaches lost
their jaunty curl, his eye its martial fire.
The dancing-school declining with the
growth of military rule in town, his occupation was chiefly to walk along the streets
picking up such rumors and crumbs of gossip
about the movements of either army as might
bring a spark of interest into the orbs of Miss
Viney on his return to the widow's house.

The days of June wore on, and Viney's
temper, taxed by anxiety about the issue of
the approaching battle, became more tart,
her taunts more frequent ; but the chevalier
suddenly seemed to take heart and to walk
with a firmer tread. One night he did not
return to sleep in his tidy bedroom, and
Viney, going into it, found a letter addressed
to herself upon the table.

"Adieu, my benefactress, beautiful inspiration of my unworthy life" (the chevalier had written), "I fly to win the approval of your noble tears or to sleep eternally upon the soldier's bloody conch. To you, in this supreme moment, I dare avow a truth for which my manhood does not blush—that I have, until now, held back because of a weakness of temperament that made my soul blanch at thought of the soldier's baptism of fire. Now that the struggle is over, I am resolved to ally myself with the armies of the South, that has given me a shelter, and given me you, adored one, whose hand I embrace in spirit, with that of your respected mother; to whom, and to you, the salutations the most distinguished of your all-devoted. ALCIBIADE."

"The land o' Dixie!" cried out Miss Viney. "If that pore crecter's in earnest I'll never draw a free breath till he gets back."

M. Alcibiade was very much in earnest. A few days later Miss Viney had a visit from a lawyer who informed her that the Frenchman, before going through the lines to enlist in the Southern army, had caused to be drawn up a will bequeathing to her some hundreds of dollars which by frugality and care he had saved during his residence beneath their roof. Viney had an honest crying-fit after the lawyer left, and, putting on her bonnet, sped down to Princess Royal Street to take counsel with the Misses Berkeley as to the best way of tracing the absent one and conveying to him some token of her appreciation and regard. Those ladies could give her little hope. They promised, however, to write recommending Alcibiade to the care and kind offices of their friends in Belhaven regiments, should the Frenchman find his way among his old acquaintances and pupils; and with this Viney was forced to be content.

After Bull Run, Manassas; and after Manassas, a breathing-space in which North and South held themselves in check, dreading to pierce the veil shadowing the future of the conflict. In the dusk of a warm summer evening, when Viney had carried out a bucket of fresh water with which to drench and cool the already clean bit of pavement appertaining to their front door, a country wagon with a hooded canopy of canvas, drawn by mules and driven by a long-legged rustic in a linen duster, wearing a broad straw hat, pulled up beside the curb. Inside could be heard the cackle of resentful fowls.

The driver, carrying a basket of eggs, leaned over and accosted her.

"No; I don't want anything to-day, I'm 'bliged to ye," began Viney — and broke down with a gasp. "Good Lord! It's you, Mounseer?"

"It is, charming Mees Viney," said the pretended farmer, with a warm grasp of her hand. "Hush! Not a word that the neighbors can overhear."

"But I don't understand; you are not in the army, after all?"

"There are ways and ways of being a soldier," he went on in a low whisper. "Believe me when I tell you I have kept my word. Take a few of these eggs and count them into a dish or basket—yes; your apron will do — that I may go on talking without fear. Then I will find it troublesome to gif you change."

"But where in the land did you come from?" she asked, burning with curiosity.

"*Ma foi*, from a Union camp, to-day, where the soldiers have left me little to sell to you, *belle dame*. To-morrow at daybreak —for I shall find fresh mules outside the town — I present myself to a general whom a Frenchman is proud to serve — ze peerless Beauregard."

"You are — you are —" she began, her face blanched, her teeth chattering.

"Never mind what I am; let me but look once more upon that face of which I so often dream, and then I must hasten away."

"Oh, go, go!" she pleaded. "It was perfect madness for you to come here. Not ten minutes ago a patrol of Yankee soldiers walked down this street."

"Bah!" he said, with a shrug, "have I not enjoyed the company of their compatriots all day? But for your sake I will go. Have no fear *belle* Viney; you will hear from me again."

Was this the timid, the cringing Alcibiade? Viney asked herself all through a sleepless night. Many and many a night thereafter she was destined to toss and wonder as to his fate. In the autumn she had a line from him, left by a wood-seller from far up in the interior of the county; he was safe and well, and still in the service of the employer who retained him when he had seen her last; and he was always her devoted and faithful A. de St. P.

After that a blank of long years extending to the close of the dreadful war.

Viney had given him up for dead, of course; had put on mourning and made her mother do the same; and everybody said how strange it was that Viney Piper should make all that fuss about a man that just walked out of her house one day and gave her the " go - by " without a word. She could never persuade herself to touch a penny of his bequest, but had consulted her confidante, Miss Penelope, about the propriety of using it for a fine monument to be erected to his memory in the Belhaven graveyard, when the correspondent of a New York paper, mousing around the old Virginia town for material, announced to the public that he had discovered the identity of the famous and daring rebel scout Peters, who, after countless adventures, and escaping the noose a dozen times by a miracle, had disappeared from sight. This dashing character, it was confidently stated, was none other than a so - called French dancing-master, known at the time as St. Pierre, who had lived in Belhaven pursuing his harmless occupation for some years prior to the war.

In the comments of the press upon this announcement more than one reminiscence of Peters was soon given currency; and presently the editor of a journal in an obscure Western town wrote to the New York

paper that Peters, *alias* St. Pierre, *alias* no-
one-knew-what beside, was then actually re-
siding in the family of a charitable Frenchman of his locality, having survived a wound
and an imprisonment that had left him helpless upon his benefactor's hands.

When this was published Viney's friends
saw the little woman smile. Then she cried,
then she fell down on her knees and thanked
God for his mercy, and lastly she packed her
little trunk, and set off for Illinois.

"You have come to me, and I was too
proud to bring the remains of me to you,
belle Viney!" said Alcibiade, when she arrived. "It is enough for me to see you, to
forget that prison where I laid so long."

Poor little, homely Viney was utterly overcome. She took his thin hand, with the
claw-like fingers, and, stooping down, kissed
it and cried over it.

"Lord, lay not this sin to my door!" she
said, gazing on the wreck before her with a
sudden, bitter self-reproach. "Oh, Mounseer,
tell me that you forgive me for what I drove
you to, for I'll never forgive myself."

"Listen to me, Mees Viney," the Frenchman said, looking about him anxiously to
see that no one overheard. "You have
done for me what a thousand times, in peril

of my neck, in cold, in hunger, in a prison cell, I have thanked you for — you have made of me a man! *Bon Dieu*, a man!''

Viney brought him back to the little chamber beneath the roof of Mrs. Piper's house, where the two women nursed him into comparative comfort; health he might never fully know again. In summer-time, his chair rolled out upon one of the shell-bordered walks, he would remain gazing in absolute content upon Viney sitting on the door-step with her work. In his eyes she was always beautiful; and when, with many misgivings, she one day consented to let Dr. Falconer, with Miss Penelope and Gay as witnesses, step into the grotto of marine curiosities and make her Madame Alcibiade, the ex-spy straightened up with something of his old dancing-master's grace.

"*Tiens!* I have won the flower of womanhood," he said. And so he thought to the last.

THE END.

www.ingramcontent.com/pod-product-compliance
Lightning Source LLC
Chambersburg PA
CBHW030105030726
47498CB00007B/2263